[untitled]

issue ten

Editorial committee

Lisa Roberts, Jess Waters, Solonge Brave, Katrina Burge, Claire Hone, Brooklyn O'Connell, Sophie Raphael, Sam Stevens, Alison Achter, Beau Hillier, Anna Bilbrough, Michaela Harden, Emma Fuelling, Meg Hellyer, Scott Vandervalk, Charlotte Long, Joey To, Laura McCluskey, Emily Whitehead

Proofreading: Daniel Car, Imogen Wishart

Cover image: Kev Howlett

Cover design: Busybird Publishing

Layout and typesetting: Busybird Publishing

Pinion Press
2/118 Para Road
Montmorency, Victoria
Australia 3094

Pinion Press is an imprint of Busybird Publishing
www.busybird.com.au

Back copies of *[untitled]* can be found on the website
www.busybird.com.au

For Blaise.

She envisioned ten issues of [untitled]
and here we are: issue ten.

Blaise was forever the champion of
emerging writers,
people who had a story they wanted to tell,
and the written word ...

1968 – 2022

Contents

Editorial

Back in 2009, the first issue of *[untitled]* was published. It began with a group of students sick of struggling to get published because we were unknown in the industry. We had big ideas. It was going to be quarterly, and we were going to change the world for new and emerging writers!

We soon realised it's not easy to publish an anthology. It's not only a lot of work, but it takes time to collect stories and then produce the book. Quarterly was reduced to twice a year, then down to yearly.

Over the past decade, we've pushed on while many other publications like this fell away due to lack of funding. We did receive a grant for issue four and that buoyed us, but mostly this still exists thanks to the ongoing voluntary work of readers and editors. We cannot underestimate how valuable this is. When you think about a few hundred stories coming in for consideration, with each one read at least twice, that's a lot of hours. I would like to thank the editorial team for this.

We've gathered the stories a little differently this year. Usually, it's by submission and the reading of 400–500 stories. For our tenth issue, we thought we'd run a competition for the whole content. All stories herein were on the longlist. It was exciting to have Laurie Steed as our judge for this issue. We think you'll enjoy the outcome.

We still believe we are the best little pocketbook of new and emerging writers in Australia. This humble anthology was an early publisher of some great Australian writers such as A.S. Patrić, Ryan O'Neill, George Ivanoff, Les Zig, Tess Evans, Laurie Steed, Laura Elvery, Koraly Dimitriadis and K.W. George (just to name a few).

It's been a tough time in the world over the past two years, but we still have stories.

We can escape to them time and again.

Happy Reading!
Blaise,
Publisher

An Open Book

Shaun Allen

He had been to this library dozens of times and he had never seen that particular door before.

It was the same as all the others – white with a single mirrored window and a round handle with keyhole, but he was sure it hadn't been here yesterday. There was no sign on the door – nothing that marked whether he could not, or should not, enter.

Curious, he glanced over his shoulder and made sure no one was around, then reached out and turned the handle. The latch clicked and he slowly opened the door, then peered down a long, empty, dark hallway. The only lights were from the space behind him. From the darkness he heard voices, muted by distance.

Stepping inside, he closed the door behind him. He took a few steps forward, then plucked up his courage and strode down the dark hall. He trailed the fingers of his left hand along the wall as his right groped about in the darkness.

For five minutes he walked until a soft light appeared ahead of him. With renewed confidence he increased his pace and reached another door the same as the one at the end of the corridor. The small window through the door was filled with light. He peered through and saw shelves of books that reached well above the height of a normal man, as hunched figures walked between them, cowled in dark, homespun cloaks.

He fumbled for the handle and twisted it until the door clicked open. Light filled the corridor and there was a cool wind that rushed forth, raising gooseflesh on his arms. He stepped into a room that reached as far he could see in either direction, with rows of shelves stretching ahead of him into the distance. Above him was a large, vaulted ceiling painted with images of saintly figures prostrating before divine light, while horrifying demons danced around flames as dark shapes burned. Along the walls, sconces burned with harsh white flame and no smoke.

One of the hunched figures rushed past him. He called out, trying to get the person's attention but they ignored him and disappeared.

He turned to the door and found that it was gone. He looked around, then spotted it a hundred metres away. He was sure he hadn't moved, but the door was clearly not behind him anymore. Sighing, he began to walk towards it only for one of the shelves to catch his eye. He hadn't noticed before, but there were faded paper tags along the shelves scribbled with names. At eye level before him, the words read *'Sharp – Sharpe'*. He ran his fingers across the tags as he felt the rough paper, marvelling at the painstaking detail in the ancient script.

He turned away from the shelf and looked back to the door, but it was gone again – this time nowhere to be seen. In each direction there were only walls covered with sconces and heavy, gold-framed paintings.

He started running. The long rows seemed to stretch back to obscurity. He ran until his breath heaved in his throat and he was forced to stop. It was there that he noticed more dark shapes scurrying between the ranks of shelves. Taking a deep breath, he began to chase after the diminutive figures, but each time he came close to one they'd disappear around a corner and vanish.

He screamed in frustration as yet another one rounded a corner and disappeared.

'Excuse me!' he called out. 'Excuse me. Can you help me?'

A tall figure appeared at the end of the row. It was draped in a heavy cloak like the rest, its face hidden by a hood pulled low. It held a thin volume close to its chest.

'Wait,' he called out, yet it turned and darted away. He watched them go, too tired now to chase any more of these strange people.

He looked around at the tattered spines of hundreds of books, with the faded text on each spine forcing him to lean close so he could examine the writing.

'Dutoit, Colleene. R 1796-1845.'

'Dutoit, Colleene. R 1854-1854.'

He wiped sweat from his forehead with his sleeve and reached for a book.

Suddenly, there was a soft, urgent voice: 'No.'

He turned and saw the tall being from before, the book still clutched tightly to its chest.

'No?' he questioned the being.

The cowled figure shook their head. 'Please. Don't touch them.' The voice was soft, feminine. They looked around urgently, then raced away.

He looked back to the books, wondering why he shouldn't take one. Walking further along the row, he stopped at a book that stuck out slightly. He looked closer.

'Dutoit, Cameron. S 1823 – 1856.'

It was the same surname. He looked back down the row, then up at the books above.

'Dutoit, Albert. J 1254 – 1256.'

This book was thin. He searched for a thicker volume and found one.

'Dutoit, Danielle. 1578 – 1655.'

'Albert was two years old. Danielle was seventy-seven years old. Are these biographies?' he whispered to himself. He reached for the larger book when his hand was slapped away.

The tall woman was back, still clutching the book to her chest. He saw a name written on the cover. *'Moore, Karina. L 1984 – 0000.'*

'You mustn't,' she hissed.

He bent down trying to see under the hood and saw a wealth of dark hair framing a pale, scared face.

'Don't touch the books. Don't open them. Don't search.' She backed away. He stood up and looked for her, but she was gone.

'Moore?' he whispered. Was it her? Was she holding a book with her name on it? Were these autobiographies?

He moved further along the shelves, looking at the names, lost in thought. An idea struck him. All along these shelves were 'D' names. He was in the wrong area. He needed 'P'.

For fifteen minutes he searched, inspecting name tags on each shelf. He had reached 'Edwards' when he sighed in frustration and started running again, with black robed shapes hissing at him as he passed.

Out of breath again, he reached his goal and was forced to lean on the shelves for support. He coughed, then straightened to look at the shelves around him. This section started at 'Pamela'. He looked about, scanning up and down. Then he found 'Paseria', then 'Pati' and 'Patongo'. He searched for five more minutes before he found 'Patrick'.

His heart beat faster in his chest as he searched, knowing with each volume he was getting closer. Looking up, he saw that the tall woman was watching him from the end of the row. She shook her head sadly, then drifted away. He stared at the empty space where she had been, then turned back to the shelves.

Suddenly there it was, right in front of him. Surely, he hadn't overlooked it – it was out of place: *'Patrick, Jason. M 1973 – 0000.'*

He looked around for the woman, but she was not in sight. Jason held out his hand and touched the spine of the volume that bore his own name. It was smaller than the others on the shelf, but still an inch thick. He placed his finger on the top of the book, then eased it out. The cover was made with blue canvas and edged in soft, brown leather.

Jason looked for a desk and sat down at one against the wall at the end of shelves, then opened the book. The first chapter he didn't understand – two unnamed people were talking in bed about the events of their day. Then, in graphic detail, it described a night of passion.

He flicked through pages, wondering what it all meant. Halfway through he found a passage that struck a chord in his memory. He read it again and again. Four boys – 'the Musketeers', they called themselves – at the school yard on a Saturday riding down the hill, jumping off their bikes and seeing which riderless vehicle rolled the furthest before crashing. 'Ghosties', they called it.

Jason slammed the book shut, pushing it away from himself. This was his memory – he remembered that day well, with old friends long forgotten. Was this volume really his life? The people making love in the first chapter – were they his parents, at the very start of his existence?

Pulling the book back, he began to read more, flicking through pages. Everything was here, his whole life. So ...?

He turned to the last page. It was filled with script, with barely any space left. He read about his hunt through the library, about the tall woman, then himself, sitting at this desk reading.

There had to be more? He turned the page and saw only the back cover. There had to be more. He wasn't dead. He was here, reading the book.

He pushed away from the desk and saw that something had been placed at the end of the desk. With a trembling hand he reached out and touched the rough, homespun fabric of a black hooded robe.

Bite

Ben Redwood

The spider appears overnight on the shelf above Alex's bed. From there, it could drop into his snoring mouth, sink its monstrous fangs into his tongue, pump him full of venom, crawl into his throat and choke him. Instead, it sews.

Alex wakes to new messages on the dating app; most importantly, one from Lydia. He opens it as he leaves the bedroom. He doesn't notice the spider, or the web spun between a photo frame and his old high-school boxing trophy. The message is timestamped midnight; she must have stayed up to send it the moment the day began.

What time should I come around? 6pm?

It's a sly way of deciding on the time while making him think the decision was his. He counters with seven-thirty. Within seconds, a barrage of replies: *cool*, then, *can't wait to see you*, then the kissing-face emoji with the love heart, an escalation from her previous use of the kissing-face with no love heart. He doesn't reply. He ignores the messages from other matches.

Lydia is something else. Pretty, kind, effervescent. The complete package. Fit, good with her hands. Full on? A tad clingy? Surely this doesn't matter, if he is willing to be clung to? Since they matched, he has considered cancelling his Platinum subscription. He barely uses the app in any serious way except to message her. He could give her his phone number. After so many years, so many failures, he sees himself reentering the ranks of the monogamous. Couple's holidays, double dates with married friends. Each day ending with the question, *How was your day?* Arguments. Reconciliations. Eternal happiness, for real this time.

Mid-afternoon, when Alex next enters the bedroom, the web covers the entire shelf: two photos in their frames frosted over like fading memories; the trophy's golden figurine mummified mid-punch;

his *Star Wars* collectable bobbleheads weighed down at the necks. Again, he fails to notice. Tiger Woods is curled up on the bed. He tickles the cat's ears, then enters the walk-in wardrobe and changes into a singlet and shorts. A message from a woman he matched with at lunchtime distracts him on his way out. He leaves it with the other unread messages. He had only been swiping out of habit.

He takes the lift to the building's gym. He is warming up before a weights session when the woman from level twenty boards the treadmill beside his. They have shared the lift several times and exchanged smiles, wider than the polite cheek-creases offered to other neighbours, but they have never spoken. The lift is always full. He continues running, upping his pace to a more impressive level, though one that will enable him to talk. She starts the conversation. They run together for forty minutes before moving to the stretching mats. He learns her name, Morgan, and her social-media handle. In the lift to their respective floors, she asks whether he has plans tonight. He almost says no. But he shouldn't disappoint Lydia. He says yes. As she steps out of the lift at the twentieth floor, he adds that he might be free tomorrow. The doors shut before she can reply.

Showered, styling his hair in the bedroom mirror, he sees the spider in the reflection. It is perched in the centre of its perfectly symmetrical web, its front legs raised as if showing off its handiwork. He drops the jar of hair product, which splatters over the glass. His throat clenches, his limbs petrify. It climbs the trophy and rappels from the figurine's fist. As if released from a spell, he bolts out of the room and slams the door behind him, grabs every tea-towel from the kitchen and stuffs them into the gap under the door. He slumps against it and tries to breath. He remembers that Tiger Woods is inside, but reassures himself that the cat will be fine, that they're born for pest control.

Still naked, he shuts the lounge-room blinds and opens the laundry cupboard. Last night's load never made it into the dryer. He starts a quick cycle, and tries to watch television while he waits, sitting on the arm of the couch next to the bedroom, pressing the toes of one foot into the tea-towels, imagining the spider pushing from the other side. Through the door, he hears the dating app's message tone. He has left his phone inside. It sounds again a few minutes later, and a few minutes after that. It must be Lydia. None of the other women are so insistent.

He wills himself to open the door a fraction. The phone's screen is lit up on the near side of the bed. Tiger Woods sleeps beside it, warming himself on

Alex's laptop as it charges. He could be in and out in five seconds. He opens it further, enough to see past the bed. The webs now extend to the adjacent wall; they must be attached to the tallboy, though he cannot see that far around. The spider is nowhere in sight. It could be anywhere. It could be above the door. He slams it and stuffs the towels back into place.

The intercom's screen shows Lydia's face, made up as if for a wedding. Opening the door for her, he recognises the floral-print sundress she purchased yesterday, according to her social-media stories. Her dark roots are freshly bleached. He hides his body behind the door, shuffling backwards as she enters until he is pressed against the wall. While she was in the lift, he'd donned grey tracksuit pants and a plain green t-shirt, both damp, because the quick cycle wasn't quick enough. His hair is splayed like a porcupine's quills. When he finally shuts the door, she looks him up and down.

'I didn't know if you still wanted me to come,' she says.

'Why would you think that?'

'You didn't answer my messages.'

'Yeah, sorry. I dropped my phone. The screen's shattered.'

They kiss, longer than a greeting, an indulgence. As their lips unlock, she grins and nips his chin, the same way Tiger Woods does. All is forgiven, although he cannot shake the thought that she read too much into a couple of unanswered messages. She stares at the dining table with a confused expression before placing her handbag on it and reaching inside. She hesitates.

'Um … do you mind if I chuck this in the bathroom?' She pulls out a toothbrush. 'Not very hygienic leaving it in here.'

He knows that denying the request will end the night immediately. He accedes. She takes the toothbrush into the bathroom.

'So, um, what's for dinner?' she calls out.

'I thought we'd get burgers.'

'Oh. You made it sound like you were cooking. Never mind.'

He wishes he could read through their messages to ascertain how he made it sound like that.

'You might have to order,' he says.

She's still in the bathroom. He wonders whether she's snooping. As if realising he would be wondering this, she pops her head around the door.

'Don't you own a laptop?'

'No. Just my phone.'

'It's fine, I can order.'

'Sorry. I'll pay you back.'

'It's no problem. Do we need wine?'

'Wine, I have.' He is thankful for the diversion. As she orders dinner on her phone, he opens a bottle and pours them each a glass. Within minutes his is empty.

'You alright?'

'Just a stressful day. With the phone breaking and everything.'

'What's everything?'

'Nothing. Really.'

'Okay. Well, try not to drink so fast. Gotta last the night.' She winks.

They attempt to find a movie that neither of them has seen. The search is suspended when the food arrives. They eat at the coffee table.

'Don't you have a cat?'

'He's sleeping.'

'Go get him. I want a pat.'

'He'll be cranky.'

'I'll risk it.'

She starts to stand. He darts his hand to her knee, and pushes himself up while holding her down. With no excuses left, he ambles over to the bedroom. He takes hold of the handle, and focuses on his breath.

'What's with the tea-towels?'

'There's a leak.'

'Under the door?'

'Running down the door.'

He opens the door, just enough to stick his head inside. He first looks up to ensure the spider isn't dangling above him, then scans the room, clenching his teeth to stop them chattering.

'He must be under the bed.'

'Just grab him already.'

'He'll scratch me.'

'Pussy.' Her tone is playful. 'I'll do it.'

'No! It's fine.'

He steps into the room. Tiger Woods hasn't moved from the laptop. Instinctively, Alex reaches for the phone beside him, but, remembering his pretence, leaves it. As he scoops his hand under the cat's belly, the sight makes him freeze.

The webs have consumed the tallboy and reached the bookshelf beside it. In the top corner of the room is a dense bundle of silk, covered by a net affixed to the ceiling and walls. He has seen such structures before: in the nature articles he has accumulated over the years in a folder on the laptop, with the unfulfilled aim of convincing himself that spiders are benign, docile, frightened of humans, dangerous only when threatened. He has seen the structures in the nightmares he suffers after reading them.

He yanks Tiger Woods off the bed and leaps out of the room. Claws sink into his forearm. He manages to slam the door just before the cat can dash inside. Tiger Woods flees into the bathroom.

Lydia laughs. 'I guess you were right! I'll get you a tissue.'

She goes into the bathroom. He presses his fingers against the holes in his arm. He hears her calling for Tiger Woods and making kissing noises. Eventually she emerges, holding the cat, but no tissue.

Well into the movie, an old Hugh Grant romcom that both of them have seen, he is clamped between Lydia and the couch's arm. Their feet are on the coffee table, playing footsies, or trying to; his remain involuntarily rigid, hers like waves slapping against a cliff. She nudges Tiger Woods off her lap and angles her body towards him; her hand crawls up his thigh, unties his tracksuit pants, slips under the waistband, and grasps him.

He can't stop thinking about baby spiders. A flood, bursting first through the tea-towels and then the whole door. How does a spider make it thirty floors up? Does it hitch a ride on the lift? Lay eggs inside a bird? Is nowhere safe? He knows the answer. One of the articles on his laptop gives the global density of spiders as one-hundred-and-thirty per square metre. The building must contain millions of them.

She has been stroking for several minutes, her coquettish smile replaced by the blank expression of an assembly-line worker. She leans in and kisses him; he reciprocates; the smile returns. Her strokes quicken; he finally hardens. She lets out a subdued moan of relief rather than pleasure, and puts her lips to his ear.

'Shall we move to the bedroom?' she whispers, before sinking her tongue into his mouth.

An image of a spider's venom-dripping fangs flashes through his mind. His whole body jolts. Lydia yanks back her head, and her hand from his pants, screams and covers her mouth. When she lowers her hand, her fingers are smeared with blood. She glares at him, mouth agape.

'What the fuck?!' Her tongue mangles the syllables.

'I'm sorry I'm sorry!'

She runs to the bathroom, and emerges holding a tissue spattered with blood.

'I'm so sorry!' he repeats.

'What the fuck is wrong with you tonight?'

'Nothing. I dunno.'

'I think I'm gonna leave.'

'Please don't. Let's watch the movie. I'm sorry.'

'No, look, I'm done for tonight.'

She ducks back into the bathroom, takes her toothbrush, and puts it in her handbag. He gets up and opens the door for her.

'Can I message you tomorrow?'

'You don't have a phone.'

He spends the night on the couch, not quite asleep but in a state of suspension until the opening of the local hardware megastore. There is a device, designed for professional exterminators, that he deploys against every spider. It is the hydrogen bomb of insecticides. If not for the walls, it could wipe out every spider on his floor. There is a crick in his neck. His thighs, tensed all night in readiness to flee, are cramped on all sides.

Lydia never leaves his not-quite-dreams. Several times during the night he finds himself looking at her profile. She's added new photos: the sundress selfie from her story; one of her jogging that he has not seen in any other media; her cheekily poking out her tongue, dripping with blood. That last one a dream, surely. He doesn't check. If he opens the app now, he will only begin swiping for her replacement. This is always the way. She clings, he swats her away, and then cannot rid himself of her.

The replacement will be compared unfavourably to her, swatted away, and so on.

Fixing his gaze downward, he sneaks into the bedroom, snatches his phone and leaves. Ordinarily, the lift ride feels like a spin of a poker machine, a ding at the twentieth floor the jackpot; but now he finds himself apprehensive at the prospect of encountering Morgan. The floor passes, and the focus of his apprehension returns to the spider. Winding his way through the internal garage, he receives a message from her. He waits until he reaches the megastore before reading it. As expected, she asks if he's free that evening.

Every time he purchases the bomb he feels embarrassed, like he is purchasing haemorrhoid cream, or creating a new account on the app after swearing himself off it forever. Why not stockpile them instead? For the same reason an addict doesn't stockpile their drug: the monotonous promise that this time will be the last. Somehow, he will react rationally next time. He will see the spider for what it is, not what he dreads it to be.

He must not leave things this way with Lydia. It's late enough in the morning that he could plausibly have put his phone in for repairs. In his *Notes* app, he composes a message explaining that the repairer had offered him a temporary replacement; apologising for feeling off last night, and vaguely alluding to some tragedy that had befallen a close friend; asking if they can try again tonight; and promising explicitly that he will cook. He gives her his phone number, acknowledging that it is well past due. After a moment weighing the consequences, he adds the kissing-face-with-love-heart emoji.

He clenches his teeth and opens the app. The profile atop his swipe stack is the sort the algorithm favours: model-gorgeous, professionally shot; likely an ad for the woman's social media, or simply a catfish. Ordinarily he would swipe right without a moment's hesitation, but not now. No replacements. No fantasies. Lydia. He opens their conversation. Her profile pic is the sundress selfie. He pastes in the message and presses send.

He replies to Morgan: *No, sorry.* Not even suggesting another time. He drives home, locks Tiger Woods in the bathroom, arms the bomb and tosses it into the bedroom. Once the blast has settled, he will need to don a mask and gloves and scrub every surface of the room, wash the bedding and all the clothes in the wardrobe. The clean-up will take more than a day. He should ask Lydia if they can meet at hers.

He opens the dating app. Her profile is gone.

Butterflies

Daniel Y. Car

I groan in relief as the heavy pack slides off my sweat-soaked shoulders. The air of the reception is cool, and the only sound is the *swish-swish-swish*ing of an old, bent-backed lady's broom as she sweeps the floor.

Peace, finally. I'm ready to collapse.

The old woman stops sweeping to look me over, her lips so tight and her eyes so narrowed that they retreat behind her dark, leathery wrinkles.

I smile and nod back. 'Hi, I'd like—'

She moves much quicker than I expect, propping her broom against the wall, shuffling around the intricate Turkish rugs and cushions and into another room.

Another woman pokes her head around the doorframe. She's younger – I guess around forty – and taller, with bright, green eyes and short, dark, wavy hair.

'Hey,' she says in an accent I can't quite place. 'Come on in.' Then she ducks back out of sight.

I lug my pack into a small room furnished with shelves and cabinets and, in the middle, a desk. The air is musty and every surface is strewn with clutter. There's no seating, so I prop my bag against the front of the desk and stand.

'So,' says the tall woman, 'what can I help you with?' She rolls up her sleeves, revealing a long scar that runs down her slim forearm.

'A bed, I hope.'

'Have you made a booking?'

'I tried calling earlier, but nobody answered.'

'Hmm …' She skims through a notebook. 'You're out of luck, I'm afraid.'

My stomach sinks.

'No free rooms – not until next week. If you'd like to book for then?'

'What can I do for tonight, though?'

'Well, we can get you a taxi to Ölüdeniz.'

I fail to hide my disappointment.

'I just got here *from* Ölüdeniz.' One night there was more than enough: *it* buzzed violently with neon light, bass-driven music, and lobsters – those boisterous, sunburnt Brits with barrel-bellies and no shirts on because it hurt too much to wear one. 'Is there anywhere else nearby?'

Her nose scrunches up in consideration, then she leans to peek back out through the doorway. It's the only way out or in, and I realise the old woman is nowhere to be seen. But she didn't squeeze out past us. 'Uh, where'd—'

The tall woman cuts me off. 'Do you have a tent?'

I pat my pack, though it's on the ground out of view. 'Yep.'

'Water?'

'I have a little left.'

'Fill up from the filter before you leave,' she says. 'It's a forty-minute hike down the cliff to Kelebekler Vadisi – Butterfly Valley, if it can still be called that. All the noise from the tourists scared the butterflies away … Anyway, you can camp on the beach there, but you'd better get going – the hike is tricky enough when there's light.'

'Okay,' I say. 'Thank you.' I try to mask the effort it takes to heft my pack back up onto my shoulders and once more walk down a path decided for me.

At the valley floor, the delicate scent of green leaves and ocean spray draws away the dusty hike's tension. A distant chillwave beat winds through the trees and vines, hinting at the direction of the campsite. I follow the music and find the reception kiosk, where a young, tanned woman is leaning back in with her bare feet crossed and kicked up on the bench.

She sits up to greet me. 'Oh, hey – here to camp?' Her accent has a hard American 'r', but not an American loudness.

'Yes. Please. Somewhere quiet if I can.'

She looks apologetic. 'It's only beach camping, and you're probably not going to get much quiet until after the bars close – that's three am.'

All the noise from the tourists scared the butterflies away.

I sign the guestbook and pay for the night in cash.

'Alright,' she says, 'you're good to go.'

'Thanks.'

'Maybe I'll see you on the dance floor later,' she adds with a wink.

'Maybe,' I say, and dispel the image of my hands on her swaying hips; I'm not much of a dancer and, besides, she probably gives the same hope to every new guest.

When I'm out of sight of the kiosk, I head away from the beachfront. I cross a wooden bridge over a murmuring stream, then step off the path. I use my phone as a torch to guide me along the stony creek bed and stop at a small clearing where the ground is mostly flat. I set up my tent, struggling to push away thoughts of the girl from the kiosk. As I crawl into my sleeping bag, I tell myself that I don't have enough room to share.

I wake up to the sound of shuffling around my tent. A goat? What else lives out here? A wild dog, maybe? Whatever it is, it says a hesitant, 'Hello?'

'Hi,' I say. My throat is parched.

'Oh,' she says. 'Somebody *is* in there.'

I swallow some water. 'Yes – I am. Can I help you?'

'Maybe,' she says, hardly louder than a whisper.

I shuffle up beside the tent wall. 'Is everything okay?'

Her voice perks up. 'With me? Yes. And you? You know, you're pretty far from the campgrounds.' Her accent is familiar.

'It's quiet here,' I say. 'I needed a good sleep.'

'Sorry,' she says. 'I was just curious, finding a tent out here.'

I yawn. 'It's fine. What time is it?'

'Does it matter? If you're tired, you should sleep.'

I unzip the tent to poke my head out. 'What time is it, though?'

'The perfect time to climb to the waterfall,' she says. She's tall, and has a white shawl draped over her shoulders. When she reaches to brush a strand of short, wavy hair away from her face, the shawl parts to a red like the desert sands back home. My eyes catch the scar on the back of her forearm.

'I know you,' I say.

Her green eyes catch the moonlight, and she smiles. 'You were at the guesthouse earlier.' She shifts her gaze to the trees and says something to herself.

'Sorry, what?'

She turns her head to me, but her eyes are fixed elsewhere. 'I should get going …'

'To the waterfall?'

Her glittering eyes lock onto mine. 'Would you like to join me?'

'What's there?'

I watch her soft lips work around the words. 'Come with me, and you can find out.'

I could go by myself in the morning, but it would be nice to have a guide.

'Just a sec',' I say, and wrestle on a shirt. When I crawl out of the tent, she offers her hand and I take it. I guess it's either my lack of sleep or the warmth of the air that makes her hand feel so light that it's hardly there at all.

For a while, only the trickling of the stream and the occasional crunching of leaves and twigs accompany our footsteps. The river cleaves the tree cover and moonlight reaches in to illuminate our path. Still, the occasional sharp thing mushes into the soles of my bare feet. She keeps glancing over her shoulder, like she's making sure I'm still there.

I follow her down into the water. It's only ankle deep, but it brings immediate relief.

'So,' she says, over the sloshing of our steps, 'tell me about yourself.'

'You first,' I say. 'I never got your name.'

'We don't need names,' she says. 'It's just us two. When we talk, we know who's addressed.'

I can't argue her logic, but I'm thrown off by her secrecy.

'What brought you to Turkey?' she says. 'To this valley – other than my recommendation.'

I watch the silver light of the stars dance on the ripples we create with each step. 'I'm not sure.' The light reflects up onto her legs and its wavering is hypnotising. What brought me here? 'Change?'

'A change that's happened, or a change you want to happen?'

I keep my eyes on her shimmering calves. 'Maybe both.'

After a moment of silence, she says, 'Go on.'

'Well … there was a girl.'

She throws her head back. 'Ha! There's always a girl.'

'Sorry to be cliché.'

She gestures with her hand. 'Continue.'

'She was excited by life, which meant she couldn't stay focused on one thing for long. I tried to be a place where she could slow down and rest but, in the end, it wasn't right for her.'

She nods. 'It's the job of the butterfly to move freely from flower to flower.'

I try to joke, 'I guess that makes me a lepidopterist,' but the words ring a little true.

'People often try to capture beautiful things,' she says, 'not realising that beauty can only ever be captured in fragments.'

I've heard similar words from musicians. It's why there are so many love songs.

'What about you?' I say. 'Do you live out here?'

She gently kicks at the surface of the water and, in that gesture, appears so much younger. 'I wish I could say "yes", but I work seasonally. I go back home in winter.'

'I guess that makes you a butterfly, too.'

She laughs.

A solitary cloud drifts over the moon and blocks its light.

She says, 'Do you know what happens to a caterpillar inside a chrysalis? It digests itself from the inside out.'

'Well, that's gross.'

'It becomes a soup of imaginal cells – meaning, of the imagination. Cells that can become anything.'

'Anything they can imagine, and they always turn into butterflies.'

'Isn't that your goal, too?' she says.

The cloud passes, and the moon lights up the water again.

'This valley is a special place; it attracts people from all over the world – often to its own detriment.'

'Beach, sun, party – it's easy to see why.'

'But none of those are the *real* reason.'

'What is the "real" reason?'

She turns to me, and her eyes flash. 'I'll show you.'

We come to a towering plateau where the river joins the base of a waterfall. The cliff face is huge, but the water only comes from about a storey up.

'It's pretty,' I say, 'but it isn't quite the awe-inspiring scene I was expecting.'

She doesn't respond, just steps right up and begins to climb using holds hidden beneath the water.

As I approach the wall, the river around my ankles grows ice-cold. When I reach to find the holds, the chill of the water knocks the air out of my lungs. I jump back to breathe.

'It's safe,' she says from above.

I look up and see her peeking over the edge of the fall.

'I promise.'

I brace myself for the shock of the water, then grip the first hold.

When I reach the top, she offers her hand again. I take it and, once more, note that it feels almost weightless. With her tug, I feel weightless, too.

I pause and look back the way we came while I catch my breath. The sky has grown ashen – the phase before sunrise, though it won't be until near midday that the sunlight reaches this part of the valley.

'It's not far now,' she says. She gestures to a knee-high tunnel behind her, carved out by the rushing water. 'We go through here.'

I bend to peer into the tunnel and a cool wind rushes out at me. The tunnel is long and steep with a pale dot of sky at the end.

She says, 'It's only accessible when the water's low. Even in the hottest summer, there's only one, maybe two days when it's safe.'

I start to shiver. 'How do you—'

'Wait until I'm through before you follow,' she says, then slides inside.

I squat and hug my knees close for warmth. I watch her but there's not enough light, nothing to see except a jostling silhouette. I smile to myself. Despite being wet and cold, there's a warmth in my chest. I've spent so much time 'sticking to the plan' and missing out. But not anymore.

Then she's through, and it's my turn. I slip into the mouth and the tunnel widens enough to crawl. I watch my hands as I lower them through the freezing water, feeling for purchase. The current threatens to sweep my feet out from under me and I can imagine the danger if the flow were any stronger.

As my vision adjusts to the dark, I can see the stalactites just above me and, off to the side, some that drip onto stalagmites like drooling fangs. I feel like I'm climbing up a demon's throat as it's trying to wash me back down.

I half-expect that she'll offer me a hand to get out when I reach the end, but nothing. I emerge, alone, into a cold, sweet-smelling fog. The air carries the sound of another waterfall more violent than the one below.

I rub my arms to warm my goose-bumped skin. 'Hello? Where are you?'

Her voice floats from somewhere ahead. 'Hurry, we're almost there.'

I jog to catch up. The mist around my ankles is so thick that I can't see the ground and I trip over a hidden root. I land on all fours beside her.

'Aren't they beautiful?' she says.

'They?' I shift into a crouch and inspect the cut on my knee. A little bloody, but not deep. I look up, and she gestures to the swirling fog. A butterfly flits down and lands on my bloody knee, and I understand that behind the mist – inside it – are countless white-winged butterflies. In my ears, the crash of the waterfall is the sound of a million delicate wings beating all at once.

'The valley was taken from them,' she says, 'but this is their sanctuary.'

'I expected something beautiful, but this—' There's so much movement that I feel dizzy.

'Come,' she says. A small cloud of butterflies accompanies each of her steps, bursting from the ground like magic and flying up to join the swarm.

'Hey, wait—' I start. Then I'm alone again.

My head feels full of air as I stand.

My knee is stiff.

I take a step and the ground shifts underfoot, so I put my arms out for balance and butterflies land on them. Butterflies crawl on my neck and my jaw. They creep over my cheeks. Their tiny feet itch, but I resist scratching for fear of hurting them, or worse. They lick at the sweat beneath my nose, so I start breathing shallow. They crawl onto my eyelids and a black tongue lashes out and hits my eye, so I shut them both. I can feel the butterflies probing at the tears in the corner of my eyes, trying to get back in.

I feel them crawling over the wound on my knee. I want to call for her, but butterfly feet tickle my lips – I picture them climbing inside the moment I open my mouth.

I focus on the sound of the waterfall and move slowly towards it, blind.

I take a step.

And another.

And—

Something grips my wrist and dispels the itching. 'We're here.'

I open my eyes and she's there, looking up at the sky. The butterflies that were crawling over me are gone, and I take a deep, satisfying breath.

We're in a small clearing, like the eye of a tornado. But it isn't weather circling us, it's a tunnel of white butterflies. Above us are the branches of a pregnant, sprawling fig tree so large that it shouldn't fit in the valley.

'No wonder they live here,' I say.

Her hold on my wrist tightens. She says, 'Did you know that butterflies are carnivorous?'

'What?'

'They like flowers and fruit, of course, but meat is a delicacy.'

The butterflies whirl around us like they're waiting.

'They wait until a body is rotten,' she says, 'until it's decayed and sweet. Then they drink up the juices.'

'Are you saying we should have brought some meat?'

There's something pitying in her smile.

I take a step backwards, her grip still locked around my wrist.

'Your butterfly girl,' she says. 'Do you know the real reason she stayed with you?'

'Huh?'

'You were so stagnant she thought you were dead. She was waiting for you to rot.'

I take another step backwards on the shifting ground.

She steps with me. 'But she got it wrong. You weren't dead: you were—'

I twist and pull my arm as hard as I can to break free from her grip.

And I do break free.

And my foot slips.

And I'm underwater.

And the white noise of the crashing waterfall becomes the rush of bubbles as they soar past my ears. The throbbing of my heartbeat, begging for air.

And the sky grows dark.

And beneath her hand, I feel so, so heavy.

She sits, cradling his head in her lap: he, with his eyes open, sightless on the jetty of bones. The fog has lifted, the butterflies have settled, and the sun has finally begun to peek into the valley. When the sunlight hits his toes, it drains the colour from his skin. As it creeps up his shins, his legs, it leaves them white as marble. His torso. When the light reaches his chest, she whispers into his ear, then lowers his lifelessness to the ground. She steps back and the sunlight engulfs him completely.

His body trembles.

His skin begins to lift by millimetres.

He delicately erupts upwards and in all directions, a flurry of desert red and corpse white.

His bones collapse under their own weight, no longer discernible from the bones of those who came before him, now hideaways for the butterflies he has become, a hundred thousand or more.

At the End of the Rainbow

Anna Miller

The crack, like a gunshot, almost shocked her off her seat at the wheel.

'GodDAMMIT!' Sara screeched into the empty studio. She wrenched the half-formed piece off the bat and flung it at the wall. The heavy thud of the clay as it hit the boards beat a bass counterpart to the tinkling aftermath of the detonation in the kiln.

This really was the limit. Sara slumped, eyes closed, hands coated in slip, while her potter's wheel spun down into silence. *It'll be that massive piece, the vase commissioned by that up- himself slimy mayor for his fancy new office*, she thought savagely. It was too big, not only destroying itself in the kiln, but taking out the batch of popular little cups and bowls destined for the farmers market up in Bell Crescent on the weekend. The tourists loved Sara's sets of brightly glazed kitchen crockery (one-of-a-kind, hand-made!) which she sold at the different country markets. If only there had been enough money to run the kiln more than once this week, she wouldn't have had to put the weekend's future takings at risk alongside that ugly-as-sin, clearly-compensating-for-something, bloody great behemoth. And that was the last of her clay stock too.

Sara sucked in air through her nose and breathed out deeply, opening her eyes. The rage departed suddenly, leaving her resigned, defeated. She glanced at the slanting afternoon sun dappling through the gum's arrow-pointed leaves outside the shabby lean-to she used as her studio. Sam would be home soon, needing a snack, needing attention. Her stool's steel feet barked sharply on the cement as she pushed herself away from the wheel, reaching for the switch which would power down the kiln. Absolutely no fricken point letting it run its full cycle now, wasting power. Sara cringed at the prospect of the now necessary begging session with Guthrie and the turn it might take. Without a further advance it would be the Foodbank for groceries next week. Tears gathered. She could already feel the mayor's greasy gaze sliding over her …

The sound of happy ten-year-old chatter intruded. Sara tugged the shed door open and crouched at the tap outside to rinse her hands. She watched the clay track runnels, like white gold, through the grass below. She breathed deeply again and smiled as Sam erupted into view along their long drive, shouting a farewell to his buddy.

'Hey, boy!' she called. 'How's the day been?'

'But I've got literally nothing to try it with! Mr Mayor, it's not just the clay, I can't afford to run the kiln—'

The Mayor of Bell Crescent grinned, his full attention on Sara, steering her towards his new office door. 'There now, Sara, you know what they say, luv: try try again,' he murmured, ostensibly leaning in to open the door for her, but coming distressingly close. 'Your grandpa made it work up there. You just gotta be a bit tougher to make it out here,' he chuckled.

'You city re-settlers are just a bit soft, but let's see what we can do to help toughen up that smooth hide of yours.' Guthrie moistened his lips as his eyes glittered over Sara's shoulders and arms, well-muscled and toned from years of working at the wheel. She felt the journey of his gaze, like a snail-trail of mucus on her skin, and shuddered. Digging her heels into the fresh beige carpet tiles, Sara tried to stop by the ugly laminate desk where the PA would soon be installed.

'Mr Mayor, let me just explain again, please.' Guthrie was reaching toward her waist, meaty hand extended. Sara sidestepped, regrettably, directly into his office.

'Now,' Guthrie let the door click shut behind him and turned the full beam of his small shark eyes on her. 'Let's see what we can do about your little problem, shall we?'

An hour later Sara sat fuming in the battered front seat of her inherited ute. All that grovelling and nothing to show. Revolting man. At least she'd gotten away without losing her cool completely – or anything else too important – and Guthrie still wanted her piece; local artist blah blah blah.

'Makes me look good to have the local stuff on display for visiting bigwigs!' Guthrie had guffawed. 'At dirt-cheap prices! Get me? Dirt-cheap!' He'd nudged up close. Ugh. She wanted nothing more than a hot shower. Or better yet, a freezing plunge in the creek at the bottom of the home paddock. Grandpa had always sworn by a creek dip to sort you out. Yes, that's next, Sara decided. She ground the gearstick into first, swearing until it engaged.

'Clutch gave out last month!' she shouted to a passing stroller-pushing mum, staring in consternation at the grating noise. The ute lurched and Sara hit the accelerator, speeding down Bell Crescent's main strip, heading for her hilly property outside of town.

It wasn't long before she was shivering, hip-deep, in the icy run-off which bubbled and sang over the pebbly bed of the home-paddock creek. Despite the day's heat, the water was cold enough to instantly raise goosebumps. *Well, Grandpa,* Sara thought, forcing herself to sink up to her neck, *this sure is one way to cure some of what ails you.*

A kookaburra chortled at her from one of the gums inclining gently over the creek. Gradually the water warmed around her. Sara drifted under the silvery boughs, her mind stilling. Cicadas droned their lullaby in the hot sun, the song of the water soothing away the day's struggles.

Suddenly, Sara splashed herself upright. 'Dirt cheap!' she exclaimed. 'Well, if you insist …'

An image of the mayor's sweaty face loomed in her memory as Sara freestyled the few strokes to the creek's edge. Flipping her wet hair from her face, she reached out to grab a handful of the mud, then dug her fingers in deeper up the bank. 'Ha! Well, at least I know where I can get my replacement stock!'

Sara clambered further away from the water's edge, smearing the flame-coloured clay along her thigh to test its consistency. 'Yep, I'll have to clean and sieve it, but this should work!'

Sara grabbed a sturdy twig from a fallen branch and began digging. *Yes,* she thought, *this will be just fine.* She'd dug a good pile when her improvised trowel struck something solid.

'What the heck—'

Sara scrabbled around, tossing grass, pebbles and muck impatiently over her shoulder.

Grandpa, she thought, *what on Earth have you left here by the creek?*

Two ripped nails, a grazed knuckle and a ripe session of swearing later, Sara uncovered the top and sides of an ancient billy can. She pulled mightily at its jammed-on lid until, with a sucking slurp and a clatter, the whole thing abruptly came free, the can and lid screeching apart.

Sara fell back, landing hard, forearm raised against the contents showering down around her. As the dust settled, Sara scrabbled upright, and froze. Still as one of her pottery pieces, she knelt in the dirt, the dust and clay like ochre war-paint on her skin. Sara gazed at the rocky nuggets scattered in the coarse grass in front of her, some shining brightly golden, others dulled brown with their exile in the tin billy.

'Grandpa! Godsakes!!'

James Bond Goes Fly-fishing

Natalie A. Vella

Seven days after.

The earth trembles beneath my feet, releasing dust and damp odours into the still air of the basement. Oscar, my carnivorous pitcher plant, jiggles in my lap. Two tapered candles illuminate the dark room like mini theatre spotlights flickering along to the tinkling wine bottles on shelves that cover the walls of the man cave. Basil's finest vino, Chateau Neuf du Pape and Bordeaux, was imported from France during our twenty-year marriage. Up until seven days ago, I never saw the inside of this underground hole. Basil's sanctuary. I'm only here because Basil is a pile of ash outside my front door.

Steel stairs lead to a small door; five centimetres of wood separate us from the toxic wasteland outside, with only a Perspex peephole as a window to the world. In the first days after the blast, my eye followed the survivors, walking zombies, passing my front gate. Flesh hanging from their bodies, they came a knock-knock-knocking on my basement door. I crouched in the corner to hide. 'Not letting them in,' I whispered, waiting until they wandered away to die.

'You're mean,' scolded my neighbour of ten years, James Bond, who, through my bad timing and his luck became my companion as the world went up in flames. But what was I going to do? Basil's office, a tiny room tucked behind the wine rack, couldn't fit any more survivors. What if they died in there? What was I going to do with their decomposing bodies?

Luckily, over the subsequent days, the number of people walking the streets dwindled and I stopped looking outside, stopped wondering if things were going to get better, stopped caring. Then the explosions and gunfire erupted. The floor quaked. Machines whizzing skywards shook the roof. Screams from whoever was left on the ground were silenced, executed by unseen bogeymen, finishing off whatever hell they had started.

James sits in his dark corner, mumbling about fishing. Again. 'Have you ever made a paper aeroplane and then threw it?' Again, with the paper plane analogy. A voice in my head screams at him, *Run the fuck out of here. Go and die with dignity.* But then another voice, a darker voice that I thought I'd locked away, whispers, *Kill him. Finish him off and be done with him.* But I can't. I won't. So I shove that voice back to the murky depths where it belongs, for the time being anyway, along with my memories of Basil.

'As I was saying, fly casting is exactly the same,' continues James. And with the snap of his wrist, he casts his rod into the middle of the room. His smile evaporates when the hook catches onto the metal stairs. He drops the rod with a huff and crawls over to retrieve it. As his chubby fingers try to unhook the lure wedged between the metal steps, he grunts, 'Nice and easy,' through gritted teeth. 'It's all in the wrist action.' With a final tug, he pulls the stubborn lure out and turns to me, proudly showing me his hook with a schoolboy grin. 'You see? You flick it, like butter.'

He walks back to the corner and begins fixing the lure. 'You see, fly casting is exactly the same as hammering a nail—'

At this point I stand up, stumbling from stiff muscles, and let out a big fat yawn to signal my boredom. My dream of Utopia with Oscar now fizzled. James mumbles something about wrist action but I tune out as I place Oscar on the bench and gently position his pitchers; creamy white with a mottled red and white lid. Such a dear little thing. The unique bulbous bottoms, filled with insect-digesting acid, seem so thin though.

I crouch down and scour behind the furniture for insects; alive or dead, but preferably alive. Anything for my Oscar, probably the last of his kind. Behind a shelf, I find the carcase of a dead fly. I suppose it will have to do. I sweep the body into my hand. Oscar waits as I open the lid of his pitcher and drop the fly in. The black dregs sink into the acid. In a day or two, the fly will have dissolved. Disappeared as if it had never existed.

Another explosion rocks the basement. Dust rises and I'm spared the rest of James's fishing lesson with a coughing fit. Today's ration of tuna in a baby-sized can threatens to surge up my food pipe. James drops his fishing rod and runs to the water supply but the little we have is all but gone. He grabs the nearest bottle of wine from the shelf, pops the cork and hands it to me. I take a swig of Basil's Chateau Neuf du Pape to stifle the choking. At first, the taste is harsh against my gravelly throat. Then its mellowed bouquet and refined palette slide down my gorge, reminding me of Basil, endlessly swirling and sniffing his glass of wine while telling me how lucky I was to have him. My cough eventually eases and after a few more swigs, my brain begins to fuzz. I wish Basil could see me now, swilling his beloved vino.

My belly is warm and for once I'm happy to be lost in a wine-induced delirium. Then James's voice breaks in. 'You gotta unroll, backstroke, forward stroke, follow through and move the fly around.' My eyes are unfocused and for a moment, he is *the* James Bond, not my dumpy fly-fishing neighbour. The Daniel Craig version of course, with his finely chiselled jaw and stubbled chin. I close my eyes to watch the fantasy unfold in my mind. I crawl over to him, lift my pretty pink dress and ride him amongst the filth and piss of this doomed room.

'Are you okay?'

I wake with a start and take my hand out of my underpants, flustered and embarrassed. James gapes at me, in disgust or shock. I'm not sure. My eyes begin to focus, sharpening to the reality that we might be here for days, weeks or years, breathing in this toxic air, our bodies decomposing together. I, a one-week widow in her pink party dress stuck with him, an overweight fly-fishing ginger. I take another gulp of wine to bring back Daniel Craig but he is long gone.

Eleven days after?

The hours and days drag between wine-fuelled sleep, inebriation and filling the plastic piss bucket in the corner. I watch over Oscar and water him with wine. He seems to thrive on it. He's thriving on something.

James picks up the fishing rod resting on his potbelly and flicks it in the air to demonstrate his swing, the fancy fly lure, with its steel hook and pigeon feathers, narrowly missing my face.

'STOP IT.' I snatch the top of the fishing pole and pull it towards me.

While I dozed, his chubby fingers must have toiled away at perfecting the feather of the fly lure.

'Let the rod go,' James protests. 'You're breaking it.'

I yank it towards me, the two of us in a tug of war, back and forth.

'Why don't you do something useful and catch something?' My hand fumbles to find his precious lure. I locate the feathery fishhook at the end of the rod and tear it from the fishing line. The rod then snaps back hitting James square in the face. He lets out a howl, which trails off into a soft whimper. Then silence.

I bury his fly in the dirt. I hope I never hear another word about fly-fishing again. My mind wanders, taking in the shapes of the room and the smell of my stinking body when I spot a cockroach scuttling along the skirting board. How on earth did it get in? I corner it, cupping it with my hands. I don't hear a peep from James. I grab a discarded wine bottle and put it in. It slides down to the bottom, its little legs moving frantically in the wine dregs. As I approach Oscar with my find, I stop short and blink, unsure if it's the two bottles of wine I drank earlier that have distorted my vision. Oscar has doubled in size. His pitchers swell in my palm. How strange. I open the lids of the other pitchers to check for insects. Nothing.

I upturn the wine bottle and drop the cockroach into the pitcher's mouth. It splashes around in Oscar's death pit, struggling to climb up the waxy wall. Eventually, it tires and drowns. Satisfied with Oscar's fill, I collapse onto my makeshift bed of dirt and with a fresh bottle of wine I begin drifting off to sleep to conjure up another fantasy.

'Where's my fly?' James blurts from the shadows, scratching his lush, ginger beard. 'Where did you put it?' With renewed vigour, he scours the earth, his harried movement sending up dust.

'What are you hoping to catch in here? Salmon?' I snap. To change the mood, I open the last can of tuna, scoff half, and offer him the rest. He ignores me, upending furniture in his quest to find his feathery thing. 'Look. It must have fallen off somewhere.' I dig up the feathered hook and throw it under the stairs while he's not looking. Maybe he will find it. Hopefully, he won't.

I raise my bottle in the air. 'To my dead husband, ashes to fucking ashes.' I gulp the remaining wine, crunchy sediment and all. My head spins on a largely empty stomach and I immediately regret guzzling all of it. I curl up into a ball and wait for the Gravitron to stop.

In a vision, I'm standing in my small greenhouse outside, on the other side of our property. The only indulgence Basil had allowed me was to keep plants. Hundreds of Nepenthes; hybrids and purebreds in all their carnivorous glory hang from their weaved baskets, their pitchers dangling low to catch predators. Sweat blisters my forehead as I stroke their leaves. Once, I found a rat floating in one of the plump pitchers. Days later, only its tail was left, the last to dissolve in the plant's acidic belly.

In the corner hangs my most prized possession, Oscar. Poached him from the vertical cliff of Mount

Kelam in Indonesian Borneo. Only a couple were left in the wild. The bulbous bottoms of the creamy white pitchers draw me in. I lift the lid, stroke his sticky ribbed rim, then I dunk my hand in, swirling the liquid. I am calm as my hand begins to dissolve and I become one with Oscar, long after the vision fades.

Um … not sure … maybe … a couple of weeks after.

I wake, wiping away chunks of crud glued to my eyes. Days may have passed. My hand tingles and dreams of Oscar fade. I've stopped counting, stopped watching the light streaming through the small Perspex. My mouth is dry, rank with wine, hunger and dehydration. With the tuna now gone, wine is our sustenance, to drink and to forget. To numb ourselves from the inevitable.

A strange silence has settled over the stench-filled basement since the bombing above ground stopped. Apart from the odd spray of gunfire, the world outside is still.

I kick up the earth, dragging my sorry self to my feet to check on Oscar. Upon lighting a match, I stagger at his size. How has he doubled again? Could it be the toxic air leaking in? I stare at my pallid skin for answers. His pitchers, now the length of my arm, are as heavy as water-filled balloons. I tip a bit of wine into his pot, turning the sphagnum moss a deep red.

Gazing into the pitcher, I catch myself dribbling. I lick my cracked lips. The liquid, so thick and delicious, looks tempting to drink. It might be a welcome break from the relentless acidity of the wine. Some indigenous cultures in Malaysia eat Nepenthes as a delicacy, stuffing it with sticky rice. But what happens when you drink it straight out of the pitcher? Would my organs dissolve? I dip my finger in and lick the nectar. It's sweet. I tip one of the pitchers into my mouth, all of it slides down my throat in seconds … Nothing.

The match burns down and I strike another to light my way, dragging Oscar behind me to Basil's office. James snores from the far corner as I push the door open and enter. I clear Basil's junk from his desk in one swipe: his inkwell, his Mont Blanc fountain pen and balls of rubber bands. Then I tenderly place Oscar down. That's when I notice a pile of papers sticking out of the drawer. I don't know why I pull them out. In bold type across the top: Application for Divorce. Basil's spider-web scrawl fills the fields as the applicant. I grip the desk to steady myself. A divorce. I pace the floor. He blindsided me. But then I stop and laugh, remembering that final moment entering his man cave. I had the last word in the end.

I rip up the papers, shove them into my mouth and chew.

'James?' My weak voice fills the room. We haven't spoken in days and my voice sounds strange. 'James, please say something?' I begin to panic. I strike my second last match. My eyes, now accustomed to the dark, hurt with the flickering flame.

After a long pause, James utters, 'Why did you take it?' There's sadness and defeat in his voice.

I sigh. 'Oh. I don't know.' The smell of filth from my skin and the stench of urine can't wash away the sudden guilt I feel for stealing his prized fishing lure.

James coughs. Unending and raw, it's a coughing tsunami that fills the room.

He struggles to breathe. I kick the wine bottles out of the way and crawl under the stairs, scouring the dirt for the fishing lure I threw there a million years ago. My hands run over the corners of the wall, over old boxes and rusting tools, sending dust into the air. After several sweeps along the ground, my hand finds what I am looking for.

I wipe the snot along my dirty sleeves and drag my withered body to James's corner. His fishing rod lies across his lap. I take his hand and place the lure in it. There is decay in the darkness and tears flow from me out of nowhere and everywhere, knowing death is close. That I had upset him.

'Go and catch your fish.' For the first time, I hold him against me. We fall asleep together.

The next day I wake up and James is gone along with his fishing rod. 'James?' I call out, my voice hoarse. He's finally gone fly-fishing. A muffled sound comes from Oscar's office. I stand up, hold my breath and listen. I approach the door and find it ajar. I don't remember leaving it open. I grab a wine bottle from the shelf and tiptoe back to the door. With my index finger, I nudge it open. The muffle sharpens to the sound of slashing. I take in a deep breath and step inside. In the gloom, I make out the outline of Oscar, his pitchers, the size of an average human, sprawling from the three-metre desk onto the floor.

I strike my last match. As the orange flame settles, the yellow glow captures the desecration in front of me. At least two of Oscar's pitchers have been hacked to pieces and his liquid pools on the dusty earth at my feet.

As I tiptoe closer, I notice James's fishing rod leaning against the wall, casually left as if awaiting his return. I run my hands over the top of the rod, the fly.

'James?' I whisper.

'You took my hook,' he replies, coolly, his mouth full. I turn towards the chewing. He never could chew with his mouth closed. 'And,' he swallows, 'you kept this plant a secret.'

The match's light captures his ginger beard, his mouth, greedily feeding on Oscar from the floor. My hand clenches and unclenches on the wine bottle as he slurps on Oscar's liquid. The dark voice returns, whispering to me, You know what to do.

'Stop. You're killing him. You're killing Oscar.'

His smug mouth continues to feast on my precious Oscar. I drop the match and smash the wine bottle over his head. The oaf sits there, frozen in shock, before keeling over on the dirt.

'Die!' I scream, hoarse and dry.

An hour later, James is floating in one of Oscar's five remaining pitchers, his ginger hair poking out from the lid, his blood darkening his final resting place. I flee the room, wheezing. I thought I'd be relieved. Instead, I scream at the scattered empty wine bottles and empty tuna cans. Scream at the corner bucket filled to the brim with shit and piss until my wracking sobs stab my ribs and I throw up red bile into the corner. In a week or two, James will be gone. Dissolved. Like he had never existed.

I grab one of the few remaining bottles of vino from the top shelf, a fine Chablis of astounding vintage, and pop its cork. Utopia is restored. Me and Oscar. Oscar and I. Together. Alone.

What day is it? It'sss the fuuuuutuuure.

An explosion of knocks splits my head in two. I peel my eyes open to the thin beam of light hitting the earth floor. It's getting harder to wake up these days. My limbs are toothpick light and chunks of my once lush hair carpet the floor.

The visitor continues to bash on the door. My head throbs. I curl up in the corner, waiting for them to leave.

'Help me,' croaks a man. A man. I huddle in my corner as he pummels the door, each kick stabbing my head.

'I know someone's there.'

My eyes widen in panic. Lifting the rags of my pink dress, I crawl, dragging my skeleton frame on all fours up the stairs to the pounding door. I pull myself up and stare out of the Perspex. An eye with spidery red veins suddenly fills the square, blocking the light.

'Let me in. Please. Let me in,' he pleads. My chest tightens. 'I won't hurt you. I promise.'

I step back from the Perspex. How does he survive the air outside? And what will happen if I open the door? He jiggles the lock. Think of Oscar, says the voice in my head. Of how ravenous he is.

My fingers tremble over the locks.

'I just want somewhere quiet. Please,' he begs.

I close my eyes, take in a long fetid breath, and unlock the first chain. The door handle continues to jiggle as I unlock the last chain. He bursts through it and I quickly slam the door shut before the toxic air enters.

With rags hanging off his jutting bones, the man crumples, sliding down the wall. 'Thank you.' Tears gush from his gaunt face.

I still don't know how he managed to survive, to breathe in that air. But I am too tired to ask. 'Don't make me regret this.'

I crawl down the metal stairs and stumble, shaving skin from my knees. When I eventually reach the bottom, I collapse from exhaustion. If the air is safe out there, it's too late for me.

The man seems to have regained his strength as he walks down the steps. But as he steps onto the earthen floor, he is overcome by the stench and keels over, vomiting up blood before collapsing in the other corner. James's corner. His face appears blistered. A gash across his forehead weeps. His skin is patches of pale yellow and red. His clothes are but strips, hanging from his wasted frame. But the colours are unmistakable. Camouflage greens and browns. Fear prickles my skin. Army.

'There's no food left so don't ask,' I mumble.

After a bout of coughing, he points to the wine shelf. 'What's that?' Without waiting for an answer, he limps over to it and takes a bottle out.

'There are not many left,' I say, clearing my throat. As he lingers next to me, I catch grease and death.

He pops the cork with nail-thin fingers and swigs half the bottle in under thirty seconds, ending the guzzle with a loud vacuous burp. 'Good shit.' He stumbles to James's corner and crashes, gulping the rest.

'What's your name?' I ask.

He scrutinises me for a moment before answering. 'Jack.'

'Well. Jack. Are you in the army?'

'Well, yes I am, ma'am.'

I clear my throat. 'What happened out there?'

'I think it's fairly obvious what happened.'

'I … I mean, what happened afterwards? I heard shooting. Explosions. Is anybody alive?'

He turns to me, real slow, the wine taking hold of him. 'Well, I can't tell you that or I'll have to kill ya.' He laughs so hard I hear a rib crack. He stops laughing and crosses his thin arms over his chest. With a moan, he closes his eyes and passes out.

I sneak past him to Oscar's office, open the door, and stare at his recovered form after James's slashing. He is now the entire length and breadth of the ten-square-metre room.

'How are you, darling?' I whisper, stroking him. I dip my hand into a pitcher and drink the liquid, just enough, before quietly exiting.

'Who's Oscar?'

I snap awake. Army man is crouched next to me, heaving his rotting breath onto my face. I panic, looking around, disorientated. Where is Oscar? How did I get back here?

'I asked you a question!' he yells in my face. 'Who's Oscar? You have somebody else hidin' in 'ere? Is that it?' He drags his fingernail across my face. 'Or is Oscar code for something?' He stands up and starts hunting around the basement, with a bottle in his hand. A new bottle from the shelf. My bottle.

'N–n–nobody. Just somebody I love very much.'

'Hmm …' he replies, unconvinced.

I count to three and stand up, pointing to the

bottle. 'What are you doing? There's only one left. You can't just—'

The force of the slap with his bony hand lights up my whole face, the sound reverberating around my head.

'What did you just say?'

I cower. 'You promised you wouldn't hurt me.'

'You promised you wouldn't hurt me,' he repeats in a mocking tone. Hand around my neck, he rubs his thumb along my windpipe. 'Didn't your mum ever tell ya to never let a strange man inside?' I push him and he lets go, holding his ribs. He takes another swig. 'This is some good shit.' He circles the room, stumbling in his shredded uniform like he owns the place.

'Well, looka here.' He points to the door of Oscar's office. 'What's in there?'

I freeze. 'In where?' I stutter.

He raises his hand, threatening to hit me. 'Don't play coy with me, little lady. What's in that room?'

'Nothing,' I stammer. 'My husband's papers. That's all.'

A grin twists the burns on his face. 'You holding out on me? You have food stashed in there?'

I lunge at him and cop a whack to my stomach for the effort. 'Get off me, bitch.'

I cry out, my retched body broken by his attack.

He opens the door. 'Whatta we have 'ere? What the hell? You've been holdin' out on me.'

I hear splashing. His grubby hands tainting Oscar.

Like a zombie, I stand up, clutching my stomach, and drag my bones to the shelf, where I take the last bottle. You know what you must do, the voice whispers. Jack, or whatever the hell his name is, doesn't know what hits him as I crack the full bottle of wine across his pathetic skull. He stumbles, stunned. It only takes a small shove for his emaciated frame to fall into Oscar's pitcher and for the first time in a very long time, I manage to smile.

Ninety-nine per cent suuuure it's Thuuuuuuursday.

I sit for an eternity in front of the cheap plywood door and remember. That day, so long ago when I stood outside that door. The earth had rumbled beneath my feet as I struggled to find the right key with one hand and held onto Oscar with the other. People were screaming. A mighty wind blew so viciously after the first bomb that the metal barbeque grill flew into the air. It danced in the eye of a mini-cyclone before it smashed against Basil's tool shed. My hands were trembling. I couldn't think, couldn't get the keys in the door's lock.

Basil was chasing me, screaming in the distance. I thought he was going to kill me. And suddenly, James was next to me. Reliable, trustworthy James. I don't remember how he arrived by my side. He snatched the keys from my hand and opened the door. The smell of sour grapes punched me in the face. Basil almost made it. He banged on the wooden door outside, begged us to let him in. For a moment, just a fraction of a second, I felt sorry for my abuser and almost relented. Almost. Through the peephole, neighbours ran and screamed with their dogs on leashes through my garden beds. Then Basil's face seized the peephole. His eyes, rimmed-red, I remember now, bulged in terror. And rage. Filled with loathing, I had turned away. Then there was another flash.

When I looked again, Basil was gone. Good riddance.

The copper door handle mocks me. *Put your hand on it and turn it. It's easy.* But my hand remains frozen at my side like a disobedient child. When the tears eventually dry, hours later, I turn to the staircase. Oscar's office is open and his monumental pitchers spill into the basement. I slump down and surrender to my fate.

It takes a while, with brittle bones, to crawl to the bottom of the stairs. The basement can't seem to contain Oscar anymore. There must be over a dozen pitchers, the size of large wheelie bins. I open a lid and the sweet scent of utopia envelopes me. I step inside and succumb to the cool liquid soaking through the thin rags that were once a pretty dress. The filth dissolves, my skin tingling as Oscar whispers comfort in the dark room and I no longer feel any pain.

Tall Trees

Nancy Podimane

Against all odds, Justice was going to plant a silver princess gum tree in the back garden of the Melbourne family home.

Her mother, who had an atavistic fear of tall trees, but had a thing about her privacy, eventually came round to the idea of a tree, but its wayward look triggered troubled thoughts.

It had bunches of red and yellow spiky flowers and weeping, silver-green foliage that shimmered and let the sun's rays dart through, which was enough to allay her mother's fear of impending darkness. But the fountain-like silhouette of the tree looked like a disorderly circus act in constant motion, even when it was perfectly still. It was a cross between a shaggy dog and a thickly powdered woman well over her prime – unshapely but dignified.

The tree, however, lulled Justice into a sense of belonging, and softened the blow of being back in the family home with its insular mindset – a ballad of courage.

Then she had a dream.

The tree was now fully grown, with thick, heavy clusters of ruby red flowers oozing nectar like a bleeding heart.

The mother stood between Justice and the tree, unaware.

'Look behind you!' The old woman's body was slow to turn.

The tree jutted into the sky, and surpassed even the clouds. The curling flakes of reddish brown bark had been transformed into the smooth, clean stem of a palm tree. Not unlike the two palm trees her father had planted when Justice and her sister were born.

'He chopped them down because they were ugly and messy. Not like the beautiful palm trees you normally see,' the mother said when Justice quizzed her.

'But they had meaning!'

'They had knobbly stems and a pathetic crown of leaves.'

'Imagine how tall they'd be by now!' pleaded Justice.

In the dream, the mother had to arch right back, bending at the knees, to take it all in. And Justice had to let go of her embarrassment, and acknowledge her feat.

When she reached the kitchen the next morning, three bulging slabs of Pangiallo baked the previous evening were waiting to be cut.

'Who cares that it's not Christmas!' the mother said, when she came up with the idea of preparing the traditional sweet.

Justice wouldn't be in Melbourne this year for Christmas, but back in Rome where she lived. The pandemic had overturned the pattern of family visits to the continent, where the parents had migrated from Italy, after the war.

'I want to bring a plate of Pangiallo to Sara and one to Giordano!' announced the mother. Good, conservative Italian kids with wholesome family values, who had never strayed from the clan. The apples of her eye. They had always been anathema to Justice and her sister, Anna, but today, Justice didn't budge. She gave in, tired of having to trash her mother's ideals and follow the family pattern of dampening one another's mood. No day would go past without them noisily colliding into each other, fragmenting the world to pieces.

Prancing around the kitchen as if she had been finally let off a leash, the mother wrapped ribbons around the sweets with a tenderness that usually made Justice feel uneasy: today she let it flow unhindered, freed of the impulse to quash it.

'Shall we take a plate of sweets next door?' Justice ventured.

They loved Jemma as family, yet she had broken the most important commandment: never abandon a person in need. And things had stayed icy ever since.

Richmond, an inner suburb where the family home stood, was full of middle-class Anglo Australians now, after the migrants had moved out. It was upmarket, quiet and aloof. Jemma, though, who had moved in with her kids straight after a tumultuous divorce, was different.

'They don't show their feelings and they're distant,' was the mother's excuse for sticking to herself. 'And they see me as a dumb immigrant!'

Justice tried to argue back, but she had her own baggage to manage.

Never quite knowing where to put her 'content' when she was back in town. People were never as forthcoming or affectionate as she wanted them to be, and she would end up at loggerheads with their emotional awkwardness. It was primarily this tendency towards disengagement that put her on edge.

'Negative thoughts are not big enough thoughts,' was the latest mantra she had stumbled on. It might help facilitate the transition from the engaging distractions of Rome to the anaesthetized tranquillity of Melbourne.

The mother lingered on the idea of a plate of sweets for Jemma. Two months had passed since her accident and she was no longer feeling sore.

'Let's do it for her kids!' she finally sentenced, landing on the perfect solution.

The mood was festive as they arranged slices of the Pangiallo on paper plates.

'What about Lucy?' probed Justice, once the feeling in the room had lightened up.

Lucy was a meek, introverted, religious woman in her 60s who lived alone. The mother found her depressing, but she had recently surprised them by turning up to the house with flowers.

'You need to build a network of people around you!' Justice insisted. 'People you can turn to in a moment of need! All your Italian friends live too far away.'

'I can't be friends with people I don't like, and are totally indifferent!' the mother ranted, as any recalcitrant adolescent would.

But she did not protest, and took out a plate for Lucy too.

'What about Marie? I know she ignored you when you were in hospital, but if we send her some sweets …'

'No! Marie, no!' There was no budging on Marie. She had not even pretended to care.

The sun was out, and the garden coming to life. While the mother went to drop off the food parcels, Justice decided to break off a branch that poked into the garden from one of the trees next door. It was making shade on the basil. She reached out with the secateurs, but it was unyielding and a struggle broke out.

Out came a fresh-faced young man from the house, whom Justice had never seen before. That was not unusual here. People moved into the neighbourhood quietly, like putting on a slipper, without a fuss or stir. No one ever seemed laden with a story to tell.

'Hello, is everything alright?' he asked.

'I'm trying to make things easier for my mum because she can't manage alone.' But the boy was not perturbed and offered to help.

'Have you just moved in?' asked Justice.

'Been here for two years now, and loving it!'

Once their battle with the branch had ended, she ran into the kitchen and wrapped four slices of Pangiallo for him.

'Your mum can knock on my door if she needs anything,' he offered with a boyish grin, as he disappeared into the house, once again enveloped in silence.

The basil, now in the sun's way, was already thriving.

'Justice! Is that you?'

Jemma's voice calling from over the fence. She had invited Jemma out for a coffee when she first arrived in Melbourne, but nothing had come of it.

'Thanks so much for the sweets. What a treat!'

She was warm and smily and Justice felt a rush of love towards her. This was the woman who had taken her mum to the hospital after she had slipped in Jemma's garden, breaking two vertebrae, and a week after the accident had suddenly stopped visiting the mother in hospital, and suspended all contact with the family.

My family comes first and I can't neglect their needs, she had written to the family, fighting off the burden of expectations, like a delusional Don Quixote.

'How have you been, Jemma?' asked Justice.

'Working too much and most of it is unpaid work, but that's my fault!' she confessed.

No word about what had passed between them.

'The good news is that I've met someone online, but the bad news is he's catfished me! He denies everything of course, but I'm so glad I noticed it straight away. Saves me bucketloads of money for the psychologist's bills!'

This was the narrative they knew: on and off, love and hate, Jemma the victim, Jemma the bully.

'He might just be busy,' Justice said in way of encouragement, and curious about this new dating lingo.

'He's a truck driver so he doesn't have much free time for me, anyway!'

'So why are you chatting with him?'

'He's got an STD and that makes it easier. I got herpes from my husband so I can't just date anyone. But I've ghosted him, now. No way is this guy going to mindfuck me. Anyway, so happy to see you sorella. I missed you!'

Nothing much had changed. This was Jemma's unfiltered, tell-all style, which the family had taken to be a sign of trust. But somewhere along the line, the signals must have got mixed up.

'She betrayed the friendship, after all the wonderful things we've shared together!' sentenced the mother, spitting out all her hurt.

But this self-righteousness began feeling stale and tiresome. All the 'good times' that had passed between them could not evidently be construed as a declaration of kinship, a promise without an exit door. And this tardy realisation did not disappoint Justice. Actually, it took a load off her shoulders.

Back from her errands, the mother was happy to learn that the ice had been broken across the fence.

The rest of the afternoon went by in a state of grace. Suspended in the air, like tightrope walkers, in a parenthesis of disbelief.

I know fuck all about people! thought Justice, who had often let disappointment be the driving force of her life.

She sat down quietly next to her mother on the garden bench, pondering over the events of the day. It had all started with the dream of the giant tree.

A moment of surrender – strong and sweet.

The harmony would not last long. They would inevitably fall back to feeling irritable and disconnected. But for one magical moment they felt whole, and in slow, perpetual expansion.

Anna, her sister in London, would be feeling it too.

And sure enough, she rang a few hours later, and they chatted about renovations to the family home. Maybe they could demolish the rundown annex. Maybe they could expand the garden, and plant more trees.

The Domovoy

Katrina Burge

Bang.
Bang.
Bang.

Yelena sobbed silently in bed, wincing with each bang from downstairs. Her husband Andrei snored loudly next to her. She dared not wake him.

The purple curtains swayed as she pulled the sheets from her thin body, placing her feet on the floor. She willed them to carry her downstairs. Confront that thing that was down there once and for all. She made a slight shuffle forward, and winced as the floorboards creaked beneath her.

The banging stopped, giving way to a sinister silence. Their bedroom sat as still as a snow leopard ready to pounce. Her breath echoed through her ears, long and rasping.

An agonised shriek tore through the house, then the slam of a door.

Yelena fell back into bed, clutching the blanket as though it were a life raft. As always, after that sickening crack, the banging stopped.

But that scream had wedged itself in her mind on repeat, vibrating through her skull. The wailing mirrored her own earlier that evening when Andrei had come barrelling towards her. What if whatever lurked in the darkness below was suffering, too?

She shook her head. She really was losing it. Somewhere between her pounding heart and Andrei's snores, she fell asleep.

Yelena lifted the crimson lid of her golden jewellery box, revealing her collection of shimmering rings. She opened the compartments and drew out a fine silver bracelet.

As she fastened the clasp around her wrist, she looked to where her husband still slept. A flashback danced across her mind: Andrei embracing her each morning, his beard tickling her forehead. Admiring her from bed as she selected her jewellery for the day. Helping her fasten her necklace and saying, 'Ya obozhaju tebya, Yelena.' *I adore you, Yelena.*

He rolled over, a hairy buttock poking out from under the satin covers. What a contrast – this regal room and bed and a giant in his slumber, waiting to unleash his wrath upon whoever dared wake him.

She admired her bracelet glinting in the sunlight that trickled under the grey clouds. A gift from Andrei in what felt like another life. A happy one. Before the pain. Before their house became a madhouse.

As she made her way downstairs, each footstep synced with the beating of her heart. It had been loud last night.

'Hello?' she called out, feeling foolish.

The kitchen, decrepit as ever, stood silent.

Still shaking, she went about her usual routine: moving the stacks of pots and pans out of the way, drawing open the curtains, and laying Andrei's plate and cutlery on the supper table in the dining room. But when she went to pick up the saucepan, it was missing. It had crashed against the stone floor yesterday after Andrei had beaten it over her head.

Drawing her arms around herself, she made her way to the cool room to grab two eggs, but could find only one. Yelena could already feel the white-hot strike of Andrei's fist against her face after placing a single egg in front of him. Her stomach swirled. Knowing her husband would still be asleep in his hungover stupor for another hour or so, she grabbed her shawl and made her way into town.

Yelena didn't need a mirror. Her bruises were reflected on every face she passed by. Some didn't even try to hide the shock. Others gave her a sympathetic glance. Those were worse. Mr Kuznetsov eyed her as she entered his grocery store. She stared at the thick black moustache hanging over his upper lip as she spoke. 'A dozen eggs, please.'

He passed the basket of eggs over the counter, giving her the same remark he always did. 'Stay safe, Yelena.'

The snow had started coming down hard, covering the dirty streets. She stopped to pull her thin shawl tighter around her shoulders. Beside her was the warmth of Ms Morozova's bookshop, dull candle light glowing through the frosted windows. Knowing there was always a warm cup of tea waiting inside for her, Yelena opened the door.

The little tinkle of a bell rang out. The smell of woody incense caressed her nose. A husky voice called out from the back of the store, 'Just one second!' There was the jingling of necklaces as her large figure appeared through the beaded doorway.

'Yelena!' she cried, nearly suffocating her in her massive bosom. Placing a polished purple finger under Yelena's chin, she examined her face and clicked her tongue in disapproval. 'My dear, my dear. I'll get the tea.'

She gestured for her to sit in front of the table, covered with a cloth that was the colour of borscht, embroidered with a swirling gold pattern. It surely cost thousands of roubles. Yelena placed the eggs down as Ms Morozova reached under the cloth and bought out a beautiful silver samovar, etchings of leaves crafted into its sides. First opening the lid to place the tea leaves inside, she then placed charcoal down the chimney and left the water to boil.

'Ms Morozova, may I talk to you about something?'

'Anything, my dear.'

'There have been … strange happenings in my house.' She chose her words carefully. Ms Morozova was a kind woman, but if she too suspected Yelena was going crazy … She shuddered at the thought.

She leaned in closer, barely audible over the sound of the water beginning to boil. 'Finding things in a different place to where I left them. Strange noises in the middle of the night. Sometimes objects disappear completely.' Her voice shook as she spoke, as much as she willed it to stop. 'I think there is a spirit in the house, and it wants to kill my husband.'

'What kind of spirit?'

It was so nonchalant, so casual. The words began to tumble from Yelena's mouth in a rush. 'It all began a few years ago. When we got pregnant, Andrei could not contain his excitement. I'd cook for him; he'd bring flowers home and tell me, "Yelena, you must be the best cook in Moscow." I'm sure you heard what happened next.

'After my miscarriage we were heartbroken. Andrei grew distant–working late as I slaved away in the kitchen. He scoffed down his food with only a belch in gratitude. It all became too much for me.' Yelena fiddled with her bracelet. 'I begged him to let us hire some servants to help out. That was the first time he struck me.'

Ms Morozova nodded, pouring the tea.

'That night, I heard crying downstairs. Like a howling dog. I woke Andrei, who snores like a boar. He could hear nothing. He told me I was crazy. And that's how it's gone on. Whenever he hurts me, come night I will hear howling, or pots and pans smashing. I have gone downstairs to find broken plates the next morning, and I hurry to clean it before Andrei wakes, lest he think it was me having an "outburst".'

Ms Morozova stared intently at Yelena. She leaned forward, her necklaces swinging back and forth.

'Have you seen the spirit?' Her voice was an enthusiastic whisper, her eyes like liquid caramel, lit up by the candles between them.

'Never. I am afraid to go downstairs when it is happening.'

Ms Morozova stood, her sandals shuffling against the thick red carpet as she disappeared through the beaded doorway.

Yelena wondered if she was going to return. Perhaps she had gone out to call the lunatic asylum and have them pick her up. She was a polite woman like that; she wouldn't have called them in front of Yelena and embarrassed her. But she shuffled back into the room, clutching an ancient-looking book. She placed it on the table, a cloud of dust lifting from the burgundy leather cover. History of the Domovoy was embossed in thick gold letters.

'This book contains the first known mention of the domovoy. Drink your tea, my dear, and I will explain.' She clasped her hands together, resting them on her large belly. 'My mother gave me this book many years ago. We lived on a farm just past Ukraine. We had lots of fine livestock. The neighbour was very jealous; his animals were sickly and thin. We weren't a rich family, but we had such good fortune.'

Her purple eye shadow glimmered as she watched her own memories as if they were dancing through the bookshop itself.

'Papa became suspicious. "Why us? Do we not feed our animals the same meals?" he wondered. Mother told him to just leave it be. But Papa did not listen, typical man he was.' She laughed. 'He hid in the barn one night where he saw a small creature feeding our horses. Papa said the only part that wasn't covered in fur were its eyes; they shone in the moonlight like dark beads. He was disgusted that such a dirty creature was contaminating our horses' food. Papa drilled a hole in the feeding trough so the creature could no longer fill it.'

Yelena rubbed a finger over the bruise on her wrist, her cold tea forgotten.

'The next morning, our animals were dead. The stable was smashed to pieces. Of course, we knew it was the creature. But we could not say anything to Papa. After that, we had no more good fortune in our house. Things went missing and got moved around.' A shadow passed over her eyes, no longer liquid caramel but dark, deep brown.

'One morning a broom was left on the floor. Papa tripped on it and broke his arm. I think it was the stress that eventually killed him. Heart attack, my dear. Mother told me then that a domovoy inhabited our house. An ancestral spirit of the household. She called him *grandfather*. "Grandfather is here to protect us," she'd say. "He lives in the stove and we must not anger him as Papa did." We asked grandfather for forgiveness for what Papa had done. Our good fortune returned, and each night we thanked grandfather.'

She opened the dusty old book, turning to a page filled with sketches of a small fur-covered creature with the face of an old man.

'This, my dear, is what inhabits your home. He seems to have taken a liking to you. But he will continue to get more aggressive until something is done. You never know when he will turn on you, too.' She waggled a wrinkled finger. 'Yelena, you must choose. Your husband or the domovoy. If you wish to live on, you must eradicate one.'

Judge's Report

Ten years is a long time in publishing.

It was ten years ago that I first contributed to *[untitled]*. Ten years on, some things have changed, but the important things have stayed the same. This journal you're holding, for example, still stands strong and continues to support emerging writers at the time when they need it the most.

With all that in mind, I was delighted to be asked to judge the *[untitled]* Short Story Competition for 2021.

Why was I so excited?

Well, you see, there's a thing about short stories that not many other forms can do, and that is channel voice, emotion and narrative velocity in a tight few thousand words.

Still, coming into the judging process, I had many questions, namely:

- *Which of these stories will provide a fresh, original take on traditional storytelling?*
- *Which will execute wholly and effectively, ensuring the arc explored is whole and deeply rewarding for the reader?*
- *Which, in my mind, is a standout story?*

While all the stories included here showed potential for publication and enjoyment, in the end, I found three stories judged first, second, and third, as follows:

- The winner of the short story competition for 2021, 'Short and Long Necks' by Jane Downing, is a truly excellent story. I was genuinely impressed by such a standout piece of absorbing, emotionally resonant fiction. All told, it was just an original, well-anchored story of resilience and redemption in a new, surprising setting.
- The second-place story, 'The Sting' by Seth Robinson, is the epitome of an engaging, accessible narrative voice. While at times a little rough around the edges, this story is so much fun and so entertaining that it's really a gift for any reader seeking freshness in their fiction. I'm not sure of the writer's current status and experience. Whatever

the case, I see a great future for anyone as effortlessly comedic and with as good an ear for dialogue as they already possess.

- The third-placed story was 'Sherry' by Jamisyn Gleeson, a simple but well-executed piece that beautifully articulates the challenges of recovery and the seductive qualities of alcohol addiction. If it sometimes makes for uncomfortable reading, that's the point. Addiction suffocates and distorts; with that in mind, I had much respect for this story's willingness to both glamorise the habit in the eyes of the protagonist while still letting the reader in on the more significant challenges ahead for one so intoxicated by escape, indulgence, and avoidance.

As for those stories not placing this time around, that mostly comes down to execution. In competition spaces, execution is everything, at least in my opinion. So, while an emerging writer might in the past have said, 'I submitted something on the off-chance it gets selected,' I say to them (in as gentle a voice as I can master), 'There is no off-chance, and if there is, you don't want it.' Which is to say that as writers we truly become great when we are in service not of ourselves, but of our stories. We excel in a competitive space when we eliminate chance, increase probability and aim to knock each and every story we write out of the park. We do that by ensuring our narrative arc is complete, that our dialogue sizzles, and that we never, ever settle for a cliché when originality is only a draft away.

With all that said, every one of the stories in this journal is well and truly worthy of commendation. Getting published is hard work, and that's really where *[untitled]* goes from being an opportunity to being a godsend. In its pages, writers find a space that says, 'You matter.' In its history, it has published stories that might otherwise struggle to find homes in Australia's diverse but ultimately academic literary culture.

Not all writers are academic, nor should they be. If you're a writer who has contributed to this book, then my hat goes off to you. If you're a reader willing to find new writers rather than being told who you should read and why then my hat goes off to you.

Why, then, should you read *[untitled]*? Because writers live here and earn their place here, not because of who they are but rather by their willingness to be brave and risk all in the pursuit of creative expression.

Your words matter. Your dreams matter. So keep going. Write stories only you can write.

And be proud, *always*.

Laurie Steed
Judge

Short and Long Necks

Jane Downing

Barb thought it was a rock at first. But it weighed little when she picked it up from the road in front of her driveway. The bloody countryside, she mumbled to herself. Closer to nature and the shells of turtles. She turned the dome over. The plastron underside was pale, a mosaic of tough segments, an armoury of irregular rectangles. The holes, or rather the entrances and exits for various limbs and body parts, loomed dark.

She carried the thing gingerly across the quiet road in front of her new house towards the reserve, holding it away from her crisply ironed shirt, which she'd chosen with great care for the day's trip into Albury.

When she'd moved in only weeks before, GoogleMaps had unreliably informed Barb there was a lake a few minutes away. She turned off the road in the direction of the putative body of water. Tarmac gave way to a path choked between scraggly natives and strappy agapanthus escaped from gardens, which then tipped into a barren, rocky moonscape. She stepped down onto the lakebed. In the distance, water shimmered, though Barb could not discount a mirage. The sun was merciless, edging reality into shadows.

She shouldn't have made the move here mid-summer; she couldn't have done otherwise with the mortgage repayments on city property crippling now she was alone. Abandoning her home of three decades had not felt like a choice. Money didn't grow on trees in a drought, or so said the graffiti in the lane beside her new local post office. She shifted the weight of the turtle and was saved from a further tumble into self-pity by the appearance of a man of about her age.

'Poor bugger,' he said from over by a stand of wattle which conferred little shade. 'Where'd you find him?'

Barb stepped back up to the shoreline, the hardened clay of the lakebed shattering into a cluster of pottery shards as her heel pressed down. She held the shell out even further from her clean shirt as if it was an offering.

'Is it alive?' she asked uncertainly.

He was squinting, the stranger, screwing more drought-ravaged river systems into the folds of his face. She reassessed the age – it was so hard to judge. He could be anywhere between fifty and seventy, in the zone which not that long ago she'd simply have labelled 'old.'

'An ex-turtle by the looks,' he said. 'Over there on the left then,' he indicated.

She shifted her gaze from the oceans of sweat on the man's striped t-shirt, a garment worn so thin with the violence of laundry-time that it had no bodily integrity of its own; so thin it was a second skin clinging to his wiry frame. To the left where he pointed, was a cairn worthy of those on the highest peaks in the neighbouring alpine region. Rock upon rock: turtle shell upon turtle shell all the way down.

Barb placed her offering at knee height. It rocked, and in finding equilibrium threatened to set off an avalanche. She held her breath, then laughed for the first time since arriving in the town. The shell popped out four leathery legs and an extraordinarily long neck and climbed off the funeral pile with commendable dignity given its skittering half-slide down.

The man of uncertain age had come to stand beside her. 'Goodness. My apologies. Well done you. A certified rescue right there.' He stuck out his hand. 'I'm Murph.'

'Barb.' She stuck out her own gritty hand for what she catagorised as a country shake – firm but embarrassed by such formalities.

'Barb,' he repeated back.

She hadn't heard her name on another's lips for so long. Too late to introduce herself by her full name as jokes from the schoolyard flooded her ears, all the Barb-wire, rough as guts, scratchy Barb, wiry perspirey Barb-wire. Her bullies had not even taken the care to be inventive.

'You really are lucky,' Murph said.

'Lucky?' She did not understand.

'They've got a scent gland above each leg. Defense mechanism. He could have squirted a real stink all over you. Somewhere between boiled cabbage and raw sewerage. Lingers for days.'

There was no real reason to have dressed in her best clothes; the procedure at the Courthouse was completely anonymous. A man came out from behind the reception's high counter, and she placed her hand on a Bible and remembered to use her full first name, and her maiden name, so the right woman did solemnly swear. The non-descript official signed as witness and it was over.

Only back in the car did Barbara realise the official had also offered a secular version of the oath for this last step in her divorce. Her nerves had pre-empted that: she'd gone for the first option and not heard him out. So in the presence of a God she no longer believed in, she signed the papers and her marriage was legally dissolved.

The crying started once she was on the highway. She had fifty minutes drive back home to the nineteenth-century rail siding that'd grown into a town. Almost an hour to recompose herself. To shake feeling back into her palm where it had rested on the Bible; to dismiss the force she'd felt coming off the leather cover as a product of her imagination. To try to distract herself with fanciful thoughts of turtle-leather book covers.

Interstate trucks growled past in the overtaking lane. Fear of their looming presence, there behind, suddenly snorting in front, eventually dried her eyes. When she got home, she decided, she'd finally look up the internet to see if there were statistics on how many couples survived the death of a child.

But she was waylaid. As she turned into the top of her street, almost home, there was another turtle. This one right in the middle of her lane. She didn't need to get out of the car to see this one was dead. The engine rattled as she sat in the stationary car unable to put her foot on the accelerator, as if the crushed shell was an insurmountable obstacle in her way.

It was not her duty to clean up. She turned off the ignition and rummaged in the boot for a couple of the thick reusable plastic bags she kept there for trips to the shops. She donned them as gloves.

A couple of circuits of the crushed shell later, she steeled herself. As she lifted, the animal inside quivered. She played statues. The movement stopped – she was the puppet master; there was no life left in the turtle to initiate action or reaction. Segments of the carapace slipped back onto the tarmac. Beneath: a dark red sirloin fleshiness.

There was a woman unloading turtle shells from a child's pull-along wagon onto the cairn when Barb got there.

'These long necks set out looking for a new habitat when the water gets low. We've scraped more than fifty off the roads in the last few weeks,' Felicity told her before introductions.

Barb's interest – about whether it was like this every year – appeared to make her worthy of an exchange of names. The whole Felicity-Barb ritual.

'Barb? Okay, call me Flick then.'

Flick was a shapeless woman, and like her partner, Murphy, was of uncertain age, though age was the operative word. The rim of her straw hat was even wider than her generous hips. Her shorts revealed dimpled knees and robust calves. She lowered her sunglasses to look more directly at Barb.

'The answer is *no* to your question.' Earnestness evaporated. 'Why don't you come out to our office?'

Barb followed her eye line and squinted across the lakebed to the mirage. A tall figure stood dark against the shimmer. She failed to find an excuse to head home.

The emptied double-layered plastic bag and former shroud had crushed down to just fit in the pockets of Barb's skirt. The pockets bulged, giving her hips Mickey Mouse ears as she followed Flick out toward the last remains of the lake. They passed flotsam exposed by the drought: whole bikes and trikes in angles of rust; the skeleton of either of these or something completely different, perhaps a golf buggy; the history of soft drink manufactures in aluminium and glass, thrown from pleasure craft in better years. Bones. Entire fish skeletons as perfect as anatomical diagrams in encyclopedias. Disinterred and scattered fragments as smooth as ivory. Dirt and dust and metres and metres of dried and cracking mud.

Looking forward not down, was equally unsettling. In the distance Murph stood beside a second child's wagon, holding upright a net on a pole. There was nothing else to catch the eye to the edges of her peripheral vision, just this whimsical image of an Edwardian butterfly collector, or, as the heat struck, a deranged homage to Burke and Wills. His head was bent down as his partner and, what Barb feared was probably the most surreal element of the scene – herself in her best outfit – trudged on into the mirage that had to be real. Or so her nose assured her.

The smell got worse and worse as they got closer to the last of the water. It wasn't only turtles losing out as nature turned on them: the fish skeletons had given the game away before the stench.

She gagged. Swallowed her revulsion at the fish stink, a smell so strong she could taste it. All smell of death had been disguised in the mortuary when she'd gone to identify her child.

At the entrance to the town's small supermarket was a sign directing shoppers to the CARP ARK. Barb hadn't been able to figure out if this was an accidental misalignment when screwing on the lettering, a deliberate mistake made by a disgruntled employee acting up, or an attempt at humour. The supermarket and its car park were the only places she went now, and only because she had to. She wished she'd gone straight home rather than follow Flick. There was no Carp Ark here; Noah had left the fish to die.

The dark figure of Murph and his fishing net cast a long afternoon shadow which met the women long before he did. Only once they were close was it clear he had his back to the shore and had not seen them coming.

He suddenly leapt forward and down went the net and up it came again with an object plucked from the shallows of the lake.

'This lot don't even have the nous to leave,' he said when he realised he had company. 'Short necks.'

Barb admired the simplicity of the categorisation. Her long neck had had a long neck, the one struggling in the net had a short neck. It also had a distinctive licorice allsorts yellow strip running from the corner of its mouth back along the side of its head.

'Can you hold the net while I get a bag?'

Barb hesitated. She wondered how she'd become part of the rescue team. She wanted to say she normally wasn't so squeamish, but these were her only good clothes. She wanted to say she needed the skirt and shirt to last because she couldn't afford more. That at the very least she feared the islands of bright blue-green would flake off, infecting her own hard shell with algae. Only, she hadn't spoken in a real conversation for so long all her words were huge in her mouth, too difficult to spit out. It was easier to comply.

'Hold firm. Don't worry, she'll pop her legs back into the limb pockets if she's worried.'

The grey leathery legs instantly did just that, the turtle transforming into the same sort of inanimate rock that had got her into this mess. It settled at the bottom of the net.

'How do you know it's a she?' Barb asked as she held onto the pole.

'He's assuming,' muttered Flick from over by the second wagon which was piled with bulky hessian bags. 'Looked like it has a pretty short tail so he's probably right.'

Murph was wetting a hessian bag, marked with the branding of a rice grower, in the murky water. A fish, a small yellowbelly, drifted on the wave he made. Drifted because it was dead.

'We haven't worked out how to effectively transport the fish,' Flick sighed

A carp ark? Barb thought but did not say aloud.

'Twenty-one years in this town and it's never been like this. We'd have worked out a system, only what's the use of a system when the environment keeps changing around us so drastically?'

The captured short neck had her legs out again by the time Murph was ready to put her in the dampened bag. They snared in the holes of the net. Barb carefully avoided her perfectly round yellow eyes.

'Little bugger,' Murph whistled. 'Doesn't know we're doing this for her own good.'

The turtle was never going to win the struggle. The limbs ripped out of the green netting, the animal fell into the bag, which was jumbled in with the other bags in the wagon.

'There'll be enough food where we're taking them,' Flick assured Barb. She must have seen the look on Barb's face. The one that said this was all too much. 'They'd starve if we left them here. No water means no food. Time to move on. They can live for thirty years, some even up to seventy-five years. This pile has got a lot of years left in them.'

The couple did not talk to each other only to her, as if decades of cohabitation had given them a silent channel of communication; or one brain to share between the two of them. Yet somehow it was decided Barb would go with them to the river, the three of them in the cab of their ute which had all the while been in the reserve's car park – correctly lettered – to the east of the cairn. Barb squashed between them on the bench seat, the gears knocking against her knees. Her stockings were already ruined.

It'd serve her right, she thought, if they turned out to be a pair of co-dependent serial killers enacting some elaborate lure to get her away from prying eyes and add her to their body count. As if she hadn't already isolated herself enough by moving away from family and friends to a town where nobody knew her story.

She didn't find out their story either, only that they weren't locals. The twenty-one years in town could not make it so. She'd have to know them for months to work out if they'd sold their farm in a once in a lifetime deal and moved into town, or if they'd done the whole tree change thing out from the city, setting up a solicitor's office or a pottery workshop or a quirky B&B, or some third scenario beyond her imagination. They were only voluble, for now, about turtles.

The locals, the real ones, they said in a conversation they obviously both knew by heart, were fatalistic. Which was a nice way of saying apathetic. They hid behind the idea that nature would take its course. As if humans had nothing to so with the lake disappearing.

Barb caught most of this above the roar of the engine and the rushing of the wind through the open windows. The landscape beyond was tinder dry: paddocks grew stubble, livestock huddled under the skirts of the occasional tree as the temperatures rose even further in the overlong afternoon, when daylight was saved, and heat banked.

Trees were taller, more closely clustered, the closer they got to the river and its many anabranches. The native grasses too were higher, but just as brittle, snapping underfoot as Barb stepped out at the hidden lagoon. It wasn't hard to see this was turtle paradise. Three, each the length of a ruler, sat sunning themselves on a fallen tree trunk in the shallows. Further out, a long neck did Loch Ness Monster impersonations above the sparkling surface. Up and under, there and gone and there again.

Barb didn't have to ask why there was enough water here, only twenty minutes from the dying lake – Murph was already telling her about the dam upstream and the periodic release of water into the river system.

Like the periodic release of the freshwater turtles, short neck and long, which commenced under their supervision. One at a time, a hessian bag was unwrapped by Murph, or Flick, and the prisoner allowed to make his or her way out, to find a path to their new habitat. This took time, minutes measured in the distance of the sun to the horizon, a filtered snapshot through stringybarks, but it was necessary for the new arrival to acclimatise even superficially.

'Letting them all go at once only seems to add to their confusion,' Flick confided quietly. 'We've learnt a lot over eighty-nine rescues.'

The next turtle's neck appeared out of the hessian weave, the first of the long neck survivors in this cargo; it could have been the one she'd found at the end of her driveway. Its throat was moving, throbbing like a frog's, a movement Barb recognised from her own silent keening over the last year and a half. Those times when the sobs were caught in her throat and could not break free. The turtle's neck swayed this way and that.

'He looks so upset,' she said, unguarded for a moment. 'I don't mean – I know you have to move them for their own sake.'

Barb wanted to cry with the long neck in this new wilderness, to cry out her pain over the newsy note that had arrived with the divorce papers. Which was worse: that her husband had the chance to start afresh, and had taken it, with a younger woman and a new child; or that he could even think a baby was a substitute for their strong son, a Worksafe statistic, a series of photos in an album still in a removalist's box, a black hole of loss in her heart?

'He's just having a bit of a smell,' Murph told her. He was perfectly still, calm and assured and reassuring as he spoke. He'd rolled up his trousers when he'd waded into the lagoon to find a good entry point, because they used a different one each day to distribute the new arrivals. His left leg was slightly bowed like an old cowboy's, his right a prosthetic extending from above the knee. She'd never have suspected. 'They have a gland in their mouth that picks up scent.' He continued. 'He's rolling the smells around in there, assessing.'

'You're making that up,' interrupted Flick from her lookout position to their left.

'No,' her partner said, but with room for doubt in the syllable. 'I read it in that thing. A gland on the roof of their mouth.'

'It's just breathing.' Flick softened. 'Don't you think?'

The turtle broke cover and headed for the water. It slipped under the surface.

Then came the next and then the next, each in its own way, in its own time. Barb watched the slow parade of the long and short necks. She allowed herself to connect with her other senses. To the itching of sweat on her skin, the cicada scratch on her eardrums. Her mouth slightly open. Smelling out the boundaries of what was left of her life.

Just continuing to breathe.

The Sting

Seth Robinson

The lift stopped with a ding, followed by a too-long pause before the doors opened. *Apparently* it was an energy saving feature – super sustainable – but it made Jeanine nervous. That pause felt just a hair longer every time, like this might be the moment the doors decided it would be more efficient to just stay closed. She might even have reached for the emergency bell if she hadn't been loaded with coffees. As such, the paper cups – not at all sustainable – saved her jumping the gun, and the accompanying embarrassment of firetrucks showing up, lights and sirens blaring. Wouldn't that be perfect? *Really* low profile.

She walked down the hall, balancing Nik's long black on top of her own cold brew as she juggled keys from her pocket. The door opened and a wave of conditioned air washed out.

'Jesus, Nik,' she muttered.

'Don't take the Lord's name in vain,' Nik called from the lounge room.

Graham Nikos was almost exclusively known as Nik, so much so that more than a few people had legitimately thought his name was Nik Nikos, which Jeanine found hilarious. She wasn't sure if he did, though. It was always hard to tell whether or not he was being serious. The 'Lord's name in vain' comment was a perfect example. Nik himself had the mouth of an amateur footy coach fresh out of rehab, but there were funny things that could get under his skin.

'It's like a walk-in freezer. You're wasting so much energy.'

'I thought this place was all greeny and sustainable?'

'That doesn't mean you just walk around turning lights on.'

She kind of doubted that anyway. It was a brutalist apartment block with loads of exposed brick and concrete, but given the dodgy lift and the subpar insulation, she thought in this case 'sustainable' might be little more than a buzzword. It wouldn't be the first time developers had jumped on the bright green bandwagon.

'They're saying it'll hit forty today. I'll take fridge over forty any day. Is that mine?' Nik took the coffee. 'Thanks.'

'So, hot coffee is your go-to for a hot day?'

'And Indian food.'

Jeanine laughed, dropped her bag, and drifted towards the set-up in the corner by the window: a kitchen stool and the DSLR on a tripod. There was a laptop and a notepad within reaching distance, along with an open packet of Burger Rings from the night before and a stack of old coffee cups. It was a plastic and cardboard memorial to the fallen soldiers of a long shift.

'Anything?' she asked.

'Nothing, but if you want to jump in, I could do with a trip to the loo.'

'Yup.'

They shuffled around each other, both keeping one eye on the yellow terrace house five stories down and across the road. They'd been staring at this particular terrace – with its rusted tin roof and cracked render – for the last three days. Personally,

Jeanine just wished someone would deal with the bins. They'd missed collection day, and now they were overflowing in the front yard.

'Give me a yell if anything happens.'

She glanced at the camera display. It was zoomed in for a tighter shot. The record icon was flashing, but all it was getting was the changing light. Nothing had happened for the last forty-odd hours. The most exciting development was an Uber Eats driver dropping off a Maccas order two days ago. After the driver left, the ground team had flagged him down and checked – it was a Big Mac meal and nuggets.

Behind her the air conditioner whirred. It was the only sound to distract her from the patter of piss on porcelain in the bathroom. Jeanine took a sip of her cold brew and let her gaze soften.

The toilet flushed, too loud in the small space, and she heard Nik turn the tap on. Internally, she started singing *Happy Birthday*. He'd better give them a good wash; she'd been sharing snacks with him all week. These were all perks though: the loaner apartment, the aircon, the bathroom. Normally stakeouts would be done in an abandoned building, or a multi-level carpark or something. It was weirdly lucky her cousin owned an apartment in this block, otherwise they never would have gotten a line of sight.

Thunk. Thunk-thunk.

She glanced up from the house. Something had bumped against the window.

The water turned off and the bathroom door opened.

Thunk.

'Hey, Jez, do you reckon we——?'

'Hold on a sec.'

Thunk. Thunk. Thunk.

Insects pattered against the glass, tumbling over the lip of the balcony above and bumbling through the air.

'What the hell?'

'Are those bees?' Nik asked.

There were dozens of them, crashing into each other, and the walls, and the glass. All completely lost.

Behind her the tone of the air conditioner shifted, changing from a ghostly hiss to an insect thrum. Jeanine glanced up and saw the first of the bees zig-zagging across the room, then a second dropped out of the open vent and onto the kitchen counter.

'Jesus!'

Nik didn't call her on it this time. He'd already snatched up the aircon remote and hit the button. It beeped loudly, a little too friendly, and the vents closed. His next move was to grab the paper on the kitchen bench and roll it, bringing it down on the counter bee in an executioner's strike.

'What the fuck? Where are they coming from?'

'Where did the other one go?' she said.

'In the bathroom, I think?'

'Shit.'

'It's alright. Just a bee.'

'I'm allergic.'

'Right. I'll get it. Stay on watch.' Nik took off, brandishing *The Age*. A moment later, she heard another papery whack. 'You're safe. I think all the windows are closed, but let me do a check!' he called from the other room.

'Thanks. Man, it's gonna get steamy in here.'

'Yep. It's gonna be a regular sauna.'

'What do we do?' she asked.

'What can we do? We've gotta stay.'

Jeanine's phone chimed. There was a new email.

Hey Jezzie,

Just got this e-mail from the BM, thought I should forward on to you. Hope it's all going well.

Cheers,
Tara

Dear Residents,

Please be aware we have run into a slight issue with the rooftop beehives and the bees have begun to swarm. Please remain calm, with your doors and windows closed and your air conditioner turned off. Residents have reported bees entering via the ventilation system.

We have contacted our apiarist, and they are on route.

Kind regards,
Building Management.

Translation: *Your overpriced, inner-city hipster haven is about to become a sweltering, 40+ degree prison cell. Have a nice day.*

PS. Bees huh? Who'd have thought something could go wrong there.

Jeanine exhaled through her teeth.

'What is it?' Nik was back, folding the newspaper up on the squashed bee carcasses. Jeanine passed the phone over, and watched his brow crumple. 'Oh, mate …'

Jeanine flicked her eyes back to the house. Still nothing. As she watched, she felt the absence of the air conditioner hiss. It had been replaced by the *rat-*

a-tat of the bees on the window. There must have been a hundred of them outside their apartment alone. How many could there have been in the hive?

'I'm gonna call the boss,' Nik said. 'Just give me a sec, I'll see what we can sort out.'

Jeanine took a swig of her cold brew, then followed it up with a stale Burger Ring. They had staying power, those Burger Rings. They tasted pretty much the same as they had the night before. Down below, the terrace house sat dormant. She was itching for something to happen, a flicker at the window, a noise complaint. Really she wanted Joel Kirney to show up – as promised – but now he was more than a day late, so even a hint of the guy would be nice. His brother's ex-wife's second cousin would be better than nothing. From the bedroom, she heard Nik speaking on the phone. There was a long pause, followed by another low exchange. The soundproofing wasn't great, either. How much did one of these places go for? This was only a one beddy so she prayed under half a mil, but these days it was hard to say. Either way, she felt like she needed to have a chat with Tara about making wiser investments.

The bloody beehives were probably a selling point.

The bedroom door opened and Nik came out.

'We have to stay. But I told him you're allergic and he's gonna try to get a shift change out. Do you go anaphylactic?'

'Yup.'

'Do you have an EpiPen?'

'I should, but nah. It's not usually a problem in the city.'

'Oh, mate.'

Jeanine shrugged. She was keeping her eyes on the terrace. There was no way she was going to miss Kirney if he showed up. 'It's alright. Honestly, I'm more worried about the heat. What are we up to now?'

Nik checked the thermometer on the outside of the air conditioner.

'26.'

'We had it set to 21, that's up five degrees in as many minutes. Bet you're regretting the hot coffee now, hey?'

Nik took a slurp. 'I can't start the day without it, doesn't matter if it's hell or high water. Here, let me get back in there.'

He'd been watching for the last hour, but Jeanine didn't mind. Nik was the senior officer, and he seemed most comfortable when he had his eyes on the prize. He'd been after Kirney for the better part of two years. It wasn't often you got a shot at one of the country's most notorious con men. Kirney had spent the last five years hustling pensioners and setting up robocall scams. Most recently, he'd managed to convince a group of wannabe property tycoons he was setting up a housing co-op and fraudulently sold them all pieces of the Werribee Tip. Why anyone would want to build on the site of an old tip was beyond her, but who knew? House prices were crazy.

Jeanine flopped down on the couch and watched a furry yellow and black body wriggle across the window. The air was thickening and her thoughts were molasses. She glanced up at the thermostat and cringed. Twenty-eight inside, and it wasn't even close to midday yet.

'I hope they get this sorted soon. Without the air—'

'Hold up. Something's happening.'

Jeanine sprang to her feet, careful to stay half-hidden behind the flapping curtain. She peeled it back from the window, trying to ignore the bees that took up most of her view.

A white Commodore had pulled up in front of the terrace house, its battered body stretched across the middle of two parking spaces. It idled for a moment, then its engine died and the driver's door popped open. The figure who hauled himself out was a beast. Well over six foot, with a rugby player's build and a bushy, black beard. He wore an oversized T-shirt and a backwards cap. Jeanine flashed a glance at the camera screen for the zoom view, but she already knew it wasn't their guy. Kirney was a ginger with the kind of sinewy build that comes from being primed and vibrating all the time.

The newcomer plodded up the front path and knocked on the terrace door. There was a pause as he scratched his belly and waited, then the door opened and a woman peered out from behind a pair of enormous sunglasses. The pair exchanged words, then the driver stooped and shuffled through the door.

'Well, not Kirney, but something.'

'That's the most action we've had all week.' Nik grabbed the notepad and scrawled the time, the car's license plate, descriptions. Jeanine glanced at her watch. 11.36am. A bead of sweat trickled down her temple, and her eyes flicked up to the thermometer. Thirty-one degrees. They'd broken into the thirties.

The big guy came out seven minutes later. He wasn't carrying anything – visibly anyway – but there would have been plenty of space under that baggy T-shirt: cash, fake IDs, maybe drugs. Kirney was an entrepreneurial type.

'Should we get a car to follow him?' Jeanine asked.

'Nah, we don't want to risk a tip off, but we'll run the plates. You mind?'

'Not at all.'

Nik passed her the notepad, and Jeanine started punching the information into the laptop. As she typed, she couldn't help but notice a slight dewiness on the keys. Her fingers were sweating.

She typed in the plate number then waited as the VicRoads database loaded. A moment later, the bushy beard and scowl of their mystery man appeared on screen.

'David Henshaw. No record. Car is registered at an address in Narre Warren.'

'That doesn't give us a lot to run with, but maybe we can pay him a visit once all this is over. Could be coincidence, but if he's one of Kirney's people he'll be worth talking to.'

'Mhmm.' Jeanine nodded. There was sweat collecting on the back of her neck, she could feel it dampening her collar. Her shirt was bunching up and gathering under her armpits, sticking to her back. She wanted to check the thermometer, to lovingly gaze upon the closed blades of the air conditioner vent, but she couldn't bring herself to do it, not again. She was becoming a masochist. She settled for a hand on the back of her neck, peeling away the sticky collar and lifting the stray strands of hair.

Beside her, Nik reached for the top button of his own shirt, then paused.

'Do you mind if I pop a couple of buttons? I've got a singlet underneath. Don't mean to be unprofessional, it's just bloody hot.'

'It's fine.'

Jeanine wished she'd worn a singlet under own shirt. She'd probably have thrown propriety aside and taken the whole thing off. As it was – on what felt like the hottest day of the year – she'd chosen flannel. What the fuck had she been thinking? The apartment was west facing. It was only going to get worse as the afternoon went on. Normally not a big deal, when you could drop the blinds and turn the AC on without risking death by anaphylaxis. And like Tara had told her, nine months out of the year, west facing windows were nice to have.

'I'm gonna … take a walk down the corridor, you mind?' Jeanine asked.

'Go for it. Just watch out for bees. Oh, and take your radio.'

Jeanine scooped her radio off the counter and clipped it onto her belt. It sat awkwardly, banging above her hip. With that and the pistol concealed at the small of her back, she didn't feel particularly undercover.

She cracked the door, checked for bees, then stepped out onto the polished concrete and blinked until her eyes adjusted to the dim hallway. It was a little cooler, *maybe,* but nowhere near enough. The whole building – scratch that, the whole suburb – was like one big kiln. It was all metal and glass and brick and concrete. It was no wonder the building was heating up. She wouldn't be too surprised if it started melting soon.

She turned away from the elevator and started a slow walk towards the end of the hall, listening to the muted tap of her shoes. The air felt wrong. Too thick, like she was wading through it. For the briefest of moments she'd hear snippets of life behind the apartment doors as she passed: the blaring of a cricket commentator, a song or an ad on the radio, muffled conversation. It was early January, so there were still plenty of people taking time off work, though they were now probably wishing they were at their air conditioned offices.

'Fuck's sake!' a man cursed from behind the nearest apartment door. From the other side of the hall Jeanine heard a loud groan. A moment later her phone chimed, and she saw another email from Tara.

Hey Jez …

Got another one from the BM. Sounds like it's a bit shit over there? Call me if there's anything I can do.

T.

Dear Residents,

Unfortunately, the apiarist will not be able to attend until later this afternoon. We are working as quickly as possible to rectify this issue. We have also called out a technician to investigate the ventilation system. As such, we request you do not turn on your aircon until we have been in touch, so we can ensure there are no larger issues.

Kind regards,
Building Management

Jeanine glanced down at her watch. 12.05. They'd made it to midday. When did the temperature usually peak? She'd always thought it was at noon, but she felt like someone had told her in the city it was more like 3:00 or 4:00pm.

From the nearest door came another muffled exchange; a man's voice, followed by a woman's. There was a nervous, agitated energy to it that made Jeanine's ears prick up.

'Hey!' the man barked sternly.

'No, don't. Leave it!' the woman replied.

There was another slurred comment from the man. Then a shriek from the woman.

Jeanine moved towards the door. Her free hand moved to her gun as she knocked.

'Police. Open the door.'

'No! Drop it! Put it down!' the woman shouted.

Jeanine stepped back, ready to kick the door in, then the handle rattled and the door swung inwards. A red-eyed man in a Carlton AFL guernsey blinked out at her. He looked frustrated, confused and a little scared, but not dangerous.

'Yes, hello. I'm sorry for the noise, we just—'

'No!' the woman screamed again, and Jeanine realised her mistake as the man pulled the door open and she heard the familiar, too friendly beep of an air conditioner. Beyond him she saw a woman, late thirties, blonde hair tied up on top of her head. It wasn't the scene of heat-induced domestic abuse Jeanine had imagined. Rather, the woman wasn't yelling at the man who had answered the door, but a boy, maybe eight or nine, who was standing half-naked and defiant on the arm of the couch, brandishing the air conditioner remote like it was a sword.

He'd hit the button and was now climbing up onto the back of the couch, stretching to keep the controller away from his reaching mother. As he did, Jeanine saw the AC vents open, fanning themselves up and down – like they were getting a feel for the room – before the unit began to issue cold air.

The first bee dropped four or five centimetres straight down, then began to fly in a mad spiral across the living room. Then there was a second, and a third. In a matter of moments there must have been more than twenty of them. The woman screamed again, this time not in anger or frustration, but with real fear and shock. The boy whirled around, dropping the remote at the same time as his dad turned away from Jeanine and swore.

'Tom, fuck!'

Jeanine lurched backwards as the first of the bees swarmed away from the panicked family and out into the hall. Jeanine ran back towards the stakeout apartment. She heard a bee buzz past her ear and ducked instinctively, stumbling as her feet tangled. Another bee landed on her arm and without thinking, she swatted at it, making to flick it away.

The pain was immediate: a sharp sting, followed by a moment of horror as Jeanine looked down and saw the bee buzzing on the back of her hand, its stinger lodged between her knuckles.

'Ah, shit!' she swore, shaking the bee loose as she staggered towards the apartment, just as another stinger found the back of her neck.

'Nik …!' Jeanine tried to yell, but it didn't meet the mark. Her throat suddenly felt itchy and tight.

People must have heard her running down the corridor because they started coming out of their apartments, then ducking away from the bees. Jeanine sat down hard on the polished concrete. She fumbled with the radio at her waist and keyed the alert button. It beeped, followed by a blast of static.

'Jez?'

The apartment door opened a crack and Nik's head popped out. As soon as he saw her, the door exploded open and he was there in the hallway.

'Have you been stung?'

Her head lolled up and down in a lackadaisical nod.

'Alright. It'll be alright. Do any of you have an EpiPen?' The last bit was shouted, and Jeanine realised it wasn't at her. It must have been at one of the residents. There were more voices. An exchange. 'Grab it! Please.'

There were still bees flying overhead. Something – the *only* thing – that Jeanine was acutely aware of. Nik must have realised as well, because a moment later he was speaking again.

'Will you help me move her? We've gotta get her away from the bees. She's allergic.'

There was more conversation, voices that sounded like they were coming from underwater, then Nik was gripping her under the armpits, and someone else had her legs. They hoisted her into the air, dangerously close to a bee that came buzzing past her nose, then moved her into the apartment. It felt like she was airborne for a lifetime, like she must have aged to the point of being decrepit, because when they set her down again it sent shock waves up her spine. There was more movement, more voices, then a sharp jab in her thigh. Another sting, ten times worse than the others. Her heart skipped a beat, then she was bolt upright, gasping in more air than her lungs could hold.

'Easy, Jez. We had to use an EpiPen.'

'Epi … I don't have …'

'It's okay, Sabrina here has a son with a peanut allergy. She let us use one of his.' Jeanine looked up and saw the worried smile of a middle-aged woman.

'Just breathe, it's alright.' Nik said. 'You're in the apartment, away from the bees. There's an ambulance on the way.'

'But what about Kirney? If he sees an ambulance …'

'It's alright. Ground team is on standby. I've got them to come around front, so if he shows—'

'The building manager is here; he says the ambulance is downstairs,' a man's voice cut in.

'Thanks. Send 'em up,' Nik said.

'Nik, you can't just write this off. You've been on Kirney for—'

'And we'll get him, but we've gotta get you sorted first. This whole thing has turned into a massive dumpster fire.' Jeanine opened her mouth, perhaps to argue – or to apologise – but he cut her off again. 'Don't worry about it. None of this is on you. Things go sideways, it happens.'

There was an electronic ding in the hallway as the lift arrived, then a male and female paramedic appeared at the door, wheeling a blue and yellow gurney. It was striped, kind of like the bees, Jeanine thought. The woman crouched down beside her and began asking her questions as Nik stood and spoke rapidly to a man in a starched shirt who she thought might have been the building manager. Nik looked mad.

'Have you had a reaction like this before?' the paramedic was asking.

'Uh, yeah, but not in a long time. At least a few years. It wasn't as bad as this.'

'Right.' She turned to the other paramedic, and they exchanged coded buzzwords, then she was back with Jeanine. 'Alright, Jeanine, we're going to get you up on the trolley here. Nice and easy, in three, two, one.' They lifted her, quick and efficient, then jacked the gurney up to its full height as they strapped her in. They covered her with a blanket to shield her from the bees, then she was being rolled out of the apartment and past the gawking neighbours who were suddenly thrilled to be hot and at home with all this drama. They wheeled her into the world's slowest lift, her and the paramedics and the building manager, who was apologising profusely to a stormy-looking Nik. Then the doors closed and they were in an even more claustrophobic space. The lift lurched into motion and suddenly the pressure was there again, making it that much harder to breathe.

'It's alright, breathe deep.' The paramedic pressed gently on the oxygen mask over her mouth and nose. She wasn't even sure when that had been placed there.

'These have to be the slowest bloody lifts in Melbourne,' Nik snarled.

The building manager opened his mouth, probably to say something about their energy saving virtues, then closed it again. There was a weighty silence as the lift eased down the shaft, then made its ceremonial pause before the doors opened again.

The paramedics wheeled Jeanine across the lobby and into the volcanic afternoon. No sooner had they crossed the threshold than Jeanine's body was drenched in sweat. The oxygen mask suddenly felt like a mini greenhouse clamped onto her face. She reached up, clawing at it, but her grip was fended off by the paramedics.

'I know, it's humid. It's alright. We'll get you in the ambulance and it'll be cooler in a second.'

They rolled her past the little café where she'd bought their coffees that morning, to where the ambulance was waiting, lights flashing. A small crowd had started to gather on the curb. Every once in a while, a car would slow down for a stickybeak.

They reached the back of the ambulance and spun the gurney around so they could slide her in head first, and she found herself looking across the street, at the terrace house. The wheels of the gurney unlocked, lifting up to the ambulance's level, and they began to push her in right as a nineties' model BMW pulled up out front. Jeanine squinted over the edge of the oxygen mask, trying to track the figure moving beyond the Beamer's windshield. She saw dark glasses and pale skin. A flash of orange hair. A moment later, the front door of the terrace opened and the woman came out, hurrying towards the car.

'Nik …' she rasped.

'Shh. Almost there—'

'Nik!' Jeanine grabbed the mask and jerked it off her face.

'Jez, you—'

'It's him! Kirney!'

Nik stiffened. His eyes flitted over to the Beamer, then back to her. The woman was over at the car now, speaking to Kirney through the open window.

'Jez …'

'You've gotta do it. Call the others. Just get him now.'

'Jeanine.' The paramedic was speaking to her again. 'We've got to get you—'

'Just wait, please.' Jeanine looked up at Nik. He nodded, then reached for the radio at his hip – turning his body so it was shielded from view – and spoke rapidly. Then he set off at a walk back up the street, so he could loop around and come from the car's rear.

'Okay Jeanine, we need—'

'One second, please.'

Jeanine forced herself up and swung around so her legs were hanging off the side of the gurney.

'Jeanine. Officer! You need to get back on the gurney now.'

'This is important,' she gasped.

She gripped the rail of the gurney, pushing away the paramedics' hands, and got herself standing. The people gathered around her were making a scene, all speaking loudly, gesturing, the two paramedics more than anyone. They were both trying to get her back on the gurney, but somehow – the adrenaline probably – Jeanine was holding them off. She could see Kirney and the woman from the terrace, both looking straight at her. The woman's mouth was in a little 'o' of confusion, and Kirney had his head cocked to one side like a dog unsure what stupidity the people were up to now. She could see Nik coming along the footpath behind the Beamer, and Hassan from the ground team coming around the corner from the laneway.

'Move,' Jeanine said, as loud as she could muster. It sounded steely, resolute, but no one was getting it.

Kirney must have caught the approach in his rearview. The car's engine revved and the woman sprang back from the window.

'Move!' Jeanine shouted, this time so loud that the nearest paramedic leapt back, more from reflex than the command.

Jeanine heaved on the side of the gurney, throwing all her weight into it. She sent it forwards, across the street as the Beamer's wheels spun. The car shot forward and at the same time Kirney must have seen the gurney rocketing towards him. He swerved, too late, shattering the gurney as the car mounted the curb and collided with the retaining wall. There was a crunch of metal on brick, then Nik and Hassan were on him, guns drawn as they dragged Kirney from the car.

'What the actual fuck?' the nearest paramedic roared, in what she was sure must have been a rare break in professionalism. But Jeanine didn't care, she was on her belly in the dirt, watching Hassan and Nik cuff Kirney. In her pocket, her phone buzzed. An email from Tara, she guessed.

She was smiling, she thought – the muscles in her face were aching in the right, smiley kind of way. But it was hard to say. Everything hurt.

'Alright,' she said. 'You can take me to the hospital now.'

Sherry

J.A. Gleeson

You imagine what the sherry will taste like in the pudding. His mother made it – the pudding with the sherry inside it. On it. Pooled around it. You try to distract yourself by thinking about what other flavours you'll be able to taste in the dessert: walnuts, crunching between molars; sticky chocolate; a slippery ganache, the texture of mud. But the imagined sugary bitterness of sherry is the flavour that sticks. It's the only liquor you've managed to stop yourself from pouring down your throat. Until now.

Well, that's not entirely true. You drank sherry as a baby. Your grandfather told you so when he was alive. Your parents gave it to you to make you quiet, to stop you from crying, to calm you down. Or so he had said. It was an old trick, passed down through generations. Your parents did it to you, your grandfather to him, and so on, and so on. You think of what it would have felt like as a child to have a fat finger dipped in sherry stick itself in your mouth as though it were a pacifier. Perhaps you thought it was one and sucked at the flesh until you drew not only sherry but also blood. Perhaps the way you suckled at that sherry as an infant was what calmed your parents, for they knew you'd have no troubles guzzling its brother and sister drinks down when you were older and in need of an inexpensive medication to soothe the pain in your brain.

You don't think you've touched sherry since. No. You imagine sliding your tongue around your mouth, licking at the solid bone of your teeth to try and savour the alcohol. You might only taste sugar – a strange sweetness you struggle to associate with liquor.

You remember the bitter taste of other drinks. The petrol-like burn down your oesophagus, the heavy warmth in your belly. Sherry isn't supposed to make you drunk. Only full. That's as it should be. It's what this family expects.

You've known your partner for about six months now. Or maybe it's a year. You can't exactly remember. Your brain is foggy, the memories stored within it cloudy. You can't decide – or maybe the proper term is *remember* – whether it's the drink's fault you've become like this or if you've purposely forgotten certain moments in your life in an attempt to start anew. When you're older, you realise how precious your youth is. You want to hold on to the string the Fates have woven for you and tease it into the length you want instead of accepting the one they've chosen. You met his parents a few months ago and have only had dinner with them a few times. You've discovered that they are good cooks and that they, like most families, eat greens for dinner before the moon rises above them and urges them to rest until morning. You feel like you're old friends with the moon. You've gazed into each other's eyes more often than you have with your own partner.

You like their fancy kitchen. The tabletops are made of marble. Or you think it's marble. You imagine it to be. Marble is fancy. Marble is nice. Better than the sticky, plasticky surfaces you grew up with. But, enough about that. More about the bowls lined up on the marble countertop. Bowls filled with sherry.

You still can't decide what colour the sherry is. In the bottle, it looked gutter-brown. Poured, a lighter oak. Yet, it isn't exactly light enough to be maple syrup, though it could be mistaken for it. Maybe you can tell your sponsor that you mistook the ingredient. That it was an innocent mistake. Surely, they'd believe you. It's not a slip if it's a mistake.

You don't know whether to reach for a spoon or a fork. Nobody has set the cutlery out yet and you feel rude opening the top drawer, where you assume they are, for yourself. You remember the sting of the slaps you received as a child for reaching for things without asking and have drilled the practice into your brain: don't reach without asking. Don't open your mouth to ask because it creates noise. Just stand and wait for instructions. Just stand and wait and don't speak, simply do, merely exist.

His mother brings out spoons and you're a little disappointed because now you don't get to watch the sticky sherry cling to the tines of a fork and slip to the bottom of the bowl as water falls through fingers. No matter. You spoon the gluggy mixture into your mouth and almost sigh at the comfort of the warmth and the familiarity of the knowledge that there is alcohol in your body once more.

Your partner looks at you. His mouth is full of pudding, his cheeks bulging from it. He looks a little like a mouse that has devoured a hunk of cheese. He looks innocent. Perhaps it is the blue of his wide eyes, or the acne scars stretching from his grin. Either way, he looks young, untouched by unhappiness. If you had children, they would be diseased by your brain. You would have to stick sherry in their mouths to stop them from crying, as infants do. And it would go on. And on.

Sometimes, you wish you were more like your partner. Or at least, you wish you were born into a family like his. You wonder if you would have ever devoured the drinks in your hands if you had been. Maybe. Maybe not. He shovels more sherry-coated pudding into his mouth. You wonder what he tastes, what he feels. If he shares your giddy excitement at the tang. Maybe. Maybe not.

And then – that's it. He packs the empty bowls into the dishwasher, where the remnants of cream and pudding and sherry that nobody could scoop into their spoons will mix in with dishwater and soap and turn into a watery muck. You feel a little like a fly, hanging around the kitchen expectantly, but his parents say their goodnights and his quiet sister slips back into her bedroom as silently as she had entered the kitchen only minutes before.

You glance at your partner, incredulous, but he only smiles back. He does not know that the cavern in your belly rumbles. He does not hear it. He has never felt it. He does not hear the ticking inside your brain, as though a bomb is about to go off inside it. He simply leads you back into his bedroom, where he tucks you into bed, under the covers on his large mattress. He does not know the way your tastebuds feel engorged whenever a wine glass is passed around a dinner table, let alone a bottle filled with the very stuff that has the power to make anyone feel detached yet uncontained. You're shocked that nobody opted to stay in the kitchen a little longer, to take a swig from the bottle. Or open another. Or share something, at least.

You just know that you feel something. And you're hoping it's not the bad kind of hollowness that almost consumed you just over a year ago.

You feel crumbs sliding against the sheets, against your legs. You don't mind them. They're comforting, in a way. They signal the fact that you'll be kept busy tomorrow, if only for a few minutes, changing the sheets, the covers, the pillowcases. Keeping your mind from things. Or trying to. He keeps the lamp on, beside the bed. It casts a warm glow over the room. Not too bright, nor dim – just enough to keep one person awake while also promising to lull the other into a sweet sleep.

You wonder what you will dream about tonight. If the dreams of broken glass and sticky floors and foamy bottle tops will haunt you. Or if you will be blessed by a dark curtain shielding your eyes from the visions of your subconscious.

In the end, though, you dream of sherry. You envision the ripe auburn colour of it and lather your naked body in it, covering every stretch mark, every burn, every scar.

You're not sure if that's a good thing or a terrible one, but you dream of it anyway. This is something that you can't control. Not quite, and not quite ever.

The Rain and the Sea

Mick Davidson

Anna watched the sky drifting by as she floated on her back across the sea's surface. She watched the seagulls and other birds slipping through the wind as it whipped the waves into life, spinning her in a lazy circle that gradually, wave by wave, took her deeper into the water, away from the beach and the world, from David.

David … the nightmare of him suffocated her during the day; in their bed she escaped from him into her dreams. But there was a time when they were joined at their souls. A time when they would plunge into bed and unbutton each other and zip themselves back together until their start and end were lost.

She'd had enough of his lies and the flickering uncertainty of his eyes. She was sick of hands that were no longer for her alone. His dry and empty lips, lips that turned kisses into lies.

It was time to end it. But not at home; she needed somewhere neutral. Their usual weekend away place by the sea seemed best. He was no swimmer, but he enjoyed the beach and the sun. She knew he'd remember their passion and delude himself into believing a weekend of pleasure would bring her back under his spell.

He had no idea how strong she could be, had no idea what she could do.

He'd think he could talk her back into her place, the space between no life and servant, where he thought he'd bought her with gifts and diamonds. A life where he was in charge. It would not be easy, she knew. He had a snake-charmer's tongue; she'd have to be prepared.

And now, while the sun was still untangling itself from the grip of the sea, she'd come down to the beach where the wind scattered her thoughts, and her doubts could drown in grey, salty waters. Waters that sustained her and whispered to her tales of a better life. A lonely, lovely place where no one came when summer passed. A place where her mind, at least, was no longer trapped in her hideous relationship.

A kittiwake followed her lazy circles, calling out to her as it skimmed along a metre or two above her head, dropping until it was almost on top of her. She saw its beak opening and closing, but from within her dream she heard only the silence of the sea.

It dropped onto her chest, twisting its head to squint its black eye into hers. It examined her face for a few moments, then took a few wet steps across her shoulder, lowered its beak into the water by her cheek and spoke. Shiny bubbles full of words floated into her ear, whispers of ancient sea-tales, shreds of faraway lands, perfect in their tranquillity, endless in their beauty. She spun in a languid circle, watching the sky greying into rain that sheeted down until the world disappeared into its folds. She stared into the greyness until she was blind from it, until her tears and the sea and the rain melted into each other, until there was no border between her and them, no separation of her atoms from the world's.

A shadow moved across her mind, a lone figure, its long stick legs pushing through the water, its hands thrust deep into pockets lost among the waves. Its old-man face looked down, searching for something in the swirl around him, his eyes moving this way and that. Then, as he bent upwards to look at her, he faded back into the waters, disappearing before she could recognise him. The figure re-emerged, face to the sea again, still pursuing the unfathomable. He stopped and looked up at her. She saw the questions written across his face, curling up out of his haggard mouth and around his liquid eyes. She saw aquamarine letters threading their way through the rain towards her. She felt their sadness and anger as they wrapped themselves around her, pulling her through the waves towards him as he sunk back into the rain and sea.

Reaching out, she grabbed the strings of words with both hands and pulled them towards her, dragging the old man out of the rain towards her. She had to see his face, to know who he was, to know what he wanted. But he dissolved away into droplets mirroring the storm gathering in her head.

She saw his words skimming over the waves, saw them snatched away by the gulls and kittiwakes who flew back to the safety of the dunes piling up along the world's edge.

The wind blew across the sands, loosening the words from beaks, dragging them up the beach and away to bury them under shattered shells. She ran after them, trapping some between her toes and splashing them down into the shallow deltas flowing home to the sea. Kneeling on the damp sand, she gathered them up into her hands, rolling them back into the story the man of the sea had whispered.

The sentences split and fractured as she forced them into her mouth, the letters ripping her lips, dripping into words that no mouth could speak, no ears could understand.

Swallowing them down, she ran into to the waves, screaming the old man's desires and dreams at him, daring him to rise again.

The words flew away but echoed back as the old man rose from waves, boiling with his rage, head straining towards her. Thunder clouds sparked across the horizon behind him. He recognised her words as his; he tasted her salty mouth on his thoughts. Knew her understanding and story. He crashed his fists into a sea that rose and fell with his breathing. The waves raced towards her, knocking her down and dragging her out towards the old man as he sank out of view.

David found her note in the kitchen: she'd rolled it up and left it in the mug she always used for his tea.

I've gone to lie down in the sea. Come and say hello. Or goodbye.

He stared down at the paper as it curled up, hiding its cryptic message.

She hadn't left his breakfast out as she normally did. He looked at the cupboard doors; what lay behind was a mystery to him. And normally that'd be too trivial for him to care about, but today … Having found some cereal and teabags, he watched the kettle working its way up to boiling point, wondering if he'd have been better off staying at home. He shouldn't have bothered with Anna, he should have let her come here by herself. He could have invited Maria over to their house instead while Anna was away. A chance missed.

'Damn you, Anna!' he shouted, smashing the spoon down into the cereal. 'I'm not even getting laid here!'

His eyes fell on the note as it lay at the other end of the table, rolling back and forth slightly, riding the vibrations of his anger. He wondered about her words.

Then he realised. She'd gone to drown herself.

Ice seized his brain and melted down into his veins.

She wanted him to find her, the bitch! She knew the trouble this would cause! There'd be the police and their questions, their expectation of explanations. And the silent, questioning looks from sympathetic friends – 'Why, David, why? But you two seemed so happy together …' His guilt stabbed and tore at his conscience, a sickening, rare and unsavoury experience. The lies, the deceptions, it was simple enough and he'd buried it all under a thick layer of pride. Pride in his cunning and ability to fool Anna it was all too easy. He stopped caring about her long ago when he found her naive trust gave him the run of the world, and the run of the prettier, younger girls.

Her name brought him back to the silent kitchen. Self-preservation kicked in: he'd have to go and stop her. Then at least no one could blame him. He'd be the hero in fact, and ruin her plan. He smiled. He was in charge again, the boss.

He dressed and hurried down to the beach through the empty autumnal lanes.

Stopping on top of the dunes, his eyes ran up and down until he saw something floating about 30 metres out, turning gently in the waves. It was Anna, she was on her back, but her face was hidden by her hair. Some kind of seabird was sitting on her chest. 'Oh God …'

He fell down the side of the dune and ran towards her, scattering gulls as he pelted across the sand. Splattering through the shallows he smashed through his fear of water. He ran out towards her, through heavier and heavier waves until, at last, they felled him and he collapsed breathless into the sea. Fighting the tide and the weight of his sodden clothes, he jerked and thrashed forwards, his lungs filling with air and water, his eyes burning with salt but always focused on her.

Then she disappeared.

He stopped and felt for the bottom with his feet, but there was nothing. His legs cycled furiously below him as he fought to keep his head above the sea. The tide welcomed him into its cold grasp.

Looking back at the beach he saw he was already a hundred metres out. He saw a figure sitting on top of the dunes. Anna? She would save him! But he had no breath to call out, just enough strength to raise an arm. He felt her eyes upon him, even as the sea dragged him further away. She waved back; surely she would help?

Something tugged at his ankle; he felt cold bony fingers gripping and digging into his flesh. Anna, the beach, and the world disappeared into a grey and speckled light. He drank in the sea, filling his belly and lungs, the water diluting his thoughts until they were no more.

Anna was sitting in the dunes when she saw David running past, heading into the sea. She watched as he splashed through the shallows, saw him crash into the water and swim away. She watched him stop and turn, saw him wave before vanishing into the grey. Her head and heart were silent: she was not inclined to save him. Her memories did not allow her to risk herself for him; there were too many thorns for that. She saw him go but did not say goodbye.

The old man rose up from where David had disappeared. He was holding something, dragging its lifeless mass through the sea as he walked out into the depths. Looking over his shoulder he waved, his bony hand scooping the clouds out of the sky.

She waved, and he was gone.

Last Days

Rosemary Dickson

Last week, I gave the nurse my brother's phone number.

'Can you tell him … No. Ask him. Just ask him to visit me? Please?' I hold no hope that he will come; that he will want to see his only brother.

Night-time. My darkened room smells of antiseptic. Silence rings in my ears; it comes high pitched, in waves. My version of silence. My companion in life. I toss and turn and listen.

The ringing crescendos as the memory of the last day of that family holiday coalesces in my mind. Dad concentrating on getting the perfect snap of the hills on his Kodak, Mum back in the car searching out our lunch, and my little brother Stevie, after I tell him to stop annoying me, toddling behind a trail of bull ants.

Shimmering heat and the smell of baking soil and eucalyptus engulfs us. Only the occasional cry of a crow cracks through the heat and the silence.

That's when I realise – at the end of the echoing cry of a crow – silence is not the absence of sound, but of external noise. I focus on the buzz inside my head until Stevie whacks me on the back with a stick, shouting, 'You're it!' I forget myself and run after him.

Maybe I should have spent more time chasing my brother.

Thoughts of that ancient summer dry out my throat. I sip water from my plastic beaker and collapse back onto the soft pillows, breathless.

Like my silence, the memories roll on, unabated.

After our picnic lunch, we arrive back at the holiday house. Dad goes for a last visit to the pub. Mum's lavender scent curls around her, lingering on the grey sofa, where she rests. The room is awash with flowers, in my nose and my mind. I know it helps her headaches. Unbidden, I bring her a glass of water. Stevie follows close behind me.

She takes the glass and rests her hot hand on mine.

'Take your brother outside. Don't come back till teatime. And no swimming.'

I nod, thinking seven must be the magic age of responsibility, of being grown up. For the first time, I'll be in charge.

Mum's voice is faint as she gives her last instruction, 'And you boys, wear hats.'

At the door, I glance back. Her eyes are closed, the circles under them greyer than lavender.

The flyscreen slaps shut behind me and Stevie.

We scramble through the ti-tree, and at the first sight of the beach we kick off our sandals, the sand burning the soles of our feet as we rush to the water's edge.

Under a huge blue sky, I stand still. The air is filled with the tang of seaweed. Soggy, rotting seaweed. I watch seagulls pecking and dancing at the water's edge, floating when the waves cover their legs. Below their folded wings and white bellies, their orange legs appear and disappear in the seaweed. Their red beaks dip and call. Without hot chips to fight over, their squawks are reduced to a burr, rising and falling with the rustling wavelets, with the hot, gusting breeze.

I pull off my cap and rub my hand over my damp hair. Mindful of Mum's instructions, I pull the cap back onto my warm head. My brother runs along the sand, the gulls rise and swirl, squawk and call, disappear from my patch of seaweed, reappear further down the empty beach. I yell sharp words to Stevie for scaring off my entertainment. He laughs and keeps running, up and down, up and down, with all the energy of his nearly three years.

I chase him through the shallows and lose all sense of time. We splash, we play tag and we make forts in the sand, decorated with feathers and shells. As the light fades, I realise we've missed our teatime. And Stevie's lost his cap.

Licking my lips, I taste salt. I drag Stevie home.

We charge inside, into the lavender house, through the slapping flyscreen.

And we see her. Our mum.

She lies sprawled on the kitchen floorboards, her chest jumping up and down, up and down. Like she's running. The skirt of her cotton dress is tangled around her knees.

We rush to her.

'Mum!'

'Mummy!'

Stevie pats her chest; I speak to her face. 'Wake up, Mum. Sorry we're late for tea.'

She says nothing. Her eyelids flutter.

I pick up her hand, it's floppy. I have to do something. I'm in charge. I stand up, 'Stevie, Stay here. I'm going to the pub. To get Dad.'

He grabs at my arm and starts crying, 'What's wrong with Mummy?'

'She's asleep. Let go.' I pull away from him. 'You stay here. With Mum.'

I run as fast as I can.

It's not fast enough.

I hold Stevie's hand at her funeral. Dad has to go up and speak, so it's just us and Aunty Sheila sitting in the front row when the Priest waves sickly sweet incense over the coffin, making Stevie cough. Tears slide down his face. I give him my hankie while Aunty Sheila digs around in her handbag. She gives us both cough lollies. I slip mine into my pocket. My throat is so tight, I'm scared I'd choke on a lolly. And then who'd look after Stevie?

Even after Stevie turns seven, I don't let him go to the pub to find Dad. That's my job. Aunty Sheila makes sure we have enough food. And I make sure we get to school on time. Stevie's job is to do his homework.

When Dad falls off a roof at work, I leave school, get a job on the trams. Aunty Sheila looks after dad, pushing him around in his wheelchair. There's no money from the compo. They say he'd been drinking.

The ringing in my ears increases with age. It hems in the thoughts in my head, stops them falling out. I am cocooned.

The day Stevie receives the notice of his scholarship to University, Dad's eyes shine like never before. He gets out the old Kodak and takes a picture of Stevie holding the letter in his hand.

The day Stevie graduates, me and Aunty Sheila can't get Dad onto the tram. Dad sits with the Kodak on his lap, and we take turns wheeling him all the way to the university. Aunty Sheila pats at her eyes with a hankie and Dad beams as Stevie marches up to accept his degree. The applause competes with the ringing in my ears, filling my head to bursting.

The day Stevie flies overseas, I volunteer to stay home with Dad. I tell Aunty Sheila to go to the airport and see Stevie off. Because she needs a break. And she'd take a better picture with the Kodak than I would.

When Aunty Sheila dies, I tell Stevie he has to come home. But he says he can't get away. He is in East Africa researching siafu, also known as driver ants or safari ants, the biggest ants in the world. So he tells us.

Dad and I bury Aunty Sheila without him.

Stevie invites us to his South African wedding, but I tell him there's no way we could make it. He should bring his bride home to meet us.

After Dad has a stroke, I speak to Stevie on an echoing overseas phone line. I tell him he needs to come back; he has to help me look after Dad. There's enough room in the house for his wife and kids. But he is writing his second book on the siafu, about their diet – usually worms or termites, though a marching column of these ants can kill and strip the flesh from small or immobilized mammals. You can't stay too still around here, he jokes. I wonder how something so small could be so powerful.

Stevie says he'll try to visit later in the year. Or early next year. His voice, with its African twang, echoes in my head; my ears buzz. He's never been home for a visit.

I tell him not to bother and end the call.

Stevie writes and asks after Dad's health. I'm sick of my brother ignoring whatever I tell him. I don't reply.

The day after Dad's funeral, I write to Stevie and tell him Dad died. His wife writes me a condolence card.

Morning. The nurse brings a tanned, balding stranger into my room. I am embarrassed at the stale cabbage smell, the fussing of the staff.

The bed dips as Stevie sits. My head rings: it chimes like a bell.

He takes my hand between his and keeps it there, his dry skin warm against mine. I drift into a doze. His hand becomes Mum's. Her warmth strengthens me.

I smell lavender and I want to weep.

I slide back to consciousness. Stevie is rubbing my shoulder. Evening has descended, and he must go.

My chest expands as he leaves, fills up with the void of his departure.

In his place, he leaves a photo of Mum holding both our hands. It's from that holiday. I lift my finger and touch the shiny surface of the photo.

My breathing slows. I taste salt, the tang of seaweed fills my senses.

I run after Stevie on the beach …

My silence rolls away.

Houseplant

Megan Howden

'Ihear you. I don't have time to waste on the day-to-day running of the family home either. The Houseplant is the ultimate household personal assistant.'

The tall, slender woman pushes open a large wooden door and steps into an expansive hall. 'I'm Chacha. Let me show you my home.' As Chacha walks down the hall, lights turn on and black ceiling fans begin to spin. She enters an enormous kitchen, luxuriously tiled, with sleek fixtures and white marble benchtops completing the look. The camera focuses on a small white pot with dangling waxy leaves, neatly situated on a shelf. Beside the plant, a small monitor is fixed to the wall. The camera frames the tendrils of the plant connecting seamlessly with the monitor.

The camera then returns its focus to Chacha, who is now standing beside the Houseplant. The camera takes in Chacha's sleek figure-hugging black jumpsuit then pans up over her ample cleavage and focuses on her smiling face; full lips, dark curly hair and blue-green eyes are set off by a smooth caramel complexion.

Chacha places her palm on the monitor beside the Houseplant.

'Welcome home,' Chacha's own voice greets her from the monitor. 'The weekly meals have been delivered, the children's bath is filling and that gift you wanted for Cam is wrapped and waiting.'

'Thanks, Alectoria,' Chacha removes her hand from the monitor and looks seductively down the lens of the camera. 'Nothing left for me to do but relax.' She winks at the camera. 'Invite us into your home today.'

'Got it in one, Chacha. We'll take it from here. You just need to do your social commitments and I reckon we've quashed the haters.'

Chacha nods at the turning back of the director. The team of statuesque crew, the makeup artists, hair dressers, camera operators, lighting and sound people, snap into action. Cases are packed, trolleys loaded and in a babbling fury they scurry to their next job.

I break the surface tension of the soapy film with my lips and nose, feeling the cool air on my wet skin, taking in a deep breath, before resubmerging my head and allowing it to rest on the bottom of the porcelain tub.

Whomp.

Whomp.

Whomp.

The blades of the black ceiling fan rotate overhead. The movement is methodical, yet on its slowest setting, the fan seems lazy. Like a child spinning with their arms outstretched, the fury and excitement of turning wildly succumbing to dizziness.

I tap my wrist and the comforting white veil slides across my vision, blocking out the fan as my mind transcends the tub. This was what it was all about, right? Creating space, making time for pleasure, technology to improve our world. I crave a break from reality just as much as the next guy. Maybe even more, because I had it all, I had you and now ...

I choose the hilltop filter. It's our hilltop. Below lies the seaside town; we knew we'd evolve, knew we could be better than our humble beginnings. From this spot we dreamed up our future. I lie on the grass, dressed in loose blue jeans and a white V-neck t-shirt. Feet bare, I feel the damp soil grounding me despite the sky and clouds spinning uncomfortably. The air pressure shifts – you are with me.

Your fingers interlock with my outstretched hand. I close my eyes, afraid that if I look you won't be there. I feel your cool flat wedding band against my skin. It's a meagre gold loop, not the ring I wanted you to have. You deserve the square-cut diamond that picked up the light from across the room. The ring that shot tiny rainbows over your skin, the kitchen sink, the roof of the car, wherever you stood the light refracted.

The day you found the bank statement you didn't say a word. Enclosing the band in its little red box, you drove me and the ring to the jewellery store. My heart broke placing that box on the cold glass counter. You smiled as you selected a band I could afford. You deserve better than me. Guess you finally realised it too.

Whomp.

Whomp.

Whomp.

The blood thumps against my eardrums.

Beautiful creatures, bronze-kissed limbs entangled on the blue net of the hammock. Your chin on my chest, the length of your torso locked against mine. My fingers lazily stroking the tresses of your beach-crimped hair. In the foreground, our fat-limbed twins, naked as the day they were born, upend shovels of powder-white sand. In the background, the pale ocean sparkles. A more perfect picture couldn't have been staged. The perfect setting, the perfect day, the perfect family, for one perfect moment.

The shot, framed and hung, was taken in one of the few rare moments of downtime while on location. I can't even remember what product the commercial was for, just that they hadn't wanted me. They wanted you, and somehow, in that way you have, you made them use me too. All morning I'd been trying to tell you what it meant to me, that faith you had in me – that faith that I probably didn't deserve. The words were so close, sitting on my lips as the photo clicked. Then the breeze picked up and sand blew into November's eyes, he cried and my moment died.

Lifting the wooden frame from the hook on the wall, I trace the outline of your neck and shoulders with my finger. This is the last piece, the jigsaw of objects that made up our life, each random shape somehow connecting neatly because it had been selected and placed by you.

I have now dismantled each part, every room of our house placed in a box. Lids taped down with directions given in fat black Texta, 'bathroom,' 'kitchen (fragile)', directions brief and purposeless. There is no home waiting like a folded-out card table for me to reassemble the puzzle upon. All that awaits our prized possessions is a storage facility in an industrial part of town.

Home, you. You, home. The two things are so tightly bound I can't untwist the thread and split it down the middle. With the frame tucked under one arm, I trace my fingers along the wall as I walk back down towards the empty kitchen.

The sleekness of this home was always smarter than I deserved but it was home because of you. Awaiting me and our children is a trundle bed at my mother's and the orange and brown decor of my childhood.

I look for you in every face, in every crowd. As the train pauses at Richmond station, the doors open and faceless bodies bustle in. Each blank face is a canvas awaiting your features. Through darkened aviators, I stare. An arched eyebrow, the bridge of a nose, hair piled like a great pompom atop a slender neck and head – there are bits of you everywhere. Parts of you sketched into this sea of strangers.

The sensation of hyperventilation takes its familiar hold. I imagine my arms scooping and dragging you towards me, but like dry white sand, each armful drawn close causes the previous to slip away. The foundations of the sandcastle were lost amongst the fine particles.

'Are you okay?'

The words swim by, buoyed along the ridges of the ocean waves. Sound waves, the voices of strangers, my ears search for any resonances that remind me of you. Tethering me back to the carpeted seat, the rocking carriage, the floor and its filthy glittering-grey lino mere inches below my face. I'm panting, panting like a dog in the heat, focusing on the black shoelaces of my sneakers.

'Get it together.' It's your voice in my brain and you're right.

Breathing in for a count of five and out for a count of five. Just like Alectoria said.

'You beings of flesh and bone, so prone to malfunction.'

The only thing that stopped me from unrooting her was that you programmed her, it was your voice.

Christ, you were smart. You could see right inside me like an MRI. You knew all my insides and how they worked. My heart descends somewhere into the location it belongs and I hide the tremor in my hands by sitting on my balled-up fists.

Sitting upright, I actually see the woman directly opposite me, a short grey skirt and matching jacket, a velvet blue headband holding back grey shoulder-length hair. The man next to her and the teenage girl next to me haven't noticed my state or the worried woman. Their eyes are glazed over with that slight milky film, the only sign that they are logged on elsewhere.

I probably knocked the woman as I collapsed onto myself, shaking her from her own program. There's concern on her features but it's mixed with fear. Bet she's wondering if I'm some kind of predator. The kind that you hear of, seeking out strangers while they're plugged in and vulnerable.

I catch a brief glimpse of myself reflected in the blackened window as the train enters a tunnel. My brown, dull, unshaven face. Unbrushed hair, flattened beneath a sweat-stained cap. Somewhere the lid for my port has been lost. The small pentagon-shaped hole, which is normally covered by a fake skin cap, is red-purple and obvious beneath my left ear. Like everyone else, I raced to get the installation. Never stopping to consider what I might be giving up. I could only see advancement and there was no way I was going to be left behind.

The woman is right to be fearful and disgusted. 'Fine. Yup, thanks,' I mumble, rising so that I can escape at the next stop.

The only thing left to do is to reset Alectoria. Crossing the kitchen, I look at the small rectangular monitor affixed to the wall above the bench. The fine white china pot containing the Houseplant remains the only evidence that a family lived in this now cavernous house. Its long waxy green leaves hang down like tentacles. The operations of the whole house are controlled from this central point.

Hmmm.

Hmmm.

Hmmm.

The Houseplant has never made a sound before. Or, perhaps, it always has but the place has never been quiet enough for me to notice. Palming the screen, the monitor warms, indicating that it recognises me.

'Afternoon, Sweets.'

How could I have forgotten this? Your voice, at once like cold water down my spine and fire in my cheeks. I tear my hand from the monitor, my breath caught in my throat. Of course, you programmed the house. It's your voice, it's your design, your imprint captured here. The task of readying the house, resetting the system for the agents, now feels like deleting you all over again. My hand shakes as I reach for the monitor again.

'What's up? Can't make your mind up? Are you coming or going?'

'I … I don't know.'

'Sweets, Sweets, Sweets, some decisions are easy. If you're staying I'll boot the place up. If you're heading out then I'll leave it as is. Don't overthink it.'

You're right. You're always right. 'I'm staying.'

'Good choice. I've made this the best place in town.'

The lights flick on, the climate control hums and down the hall, I can hear the tub filling. 'I don't deserve you.'

'Ha, maybe not, but you got me. I see there's no food in the fridge. I'll order in while you soak in the tub.'

I hesitate. 'I've got to get back to the kids.'

'Sweets, your mother's looking after them. It's all arranged.'

Her voice fills the space, fills me. This is our home and I want it to be our home for a little while longer, so I play along.

'Just us two?'

'Yeah, just you and me, Sweets. I'll order from the fancy place.'

I take my hand from the monitor.

The tone sounds in my head. It's the only feature I can't seem to shut off. I know who it'll be, of course: Mother, trying to contact me for the fourth time today. I found a patch that diverts all messages to some message bank in Pakistan. So, I don't have to hear her voice but I can imagine what she'll say, 'Your children need you. I'm their grandmother, not their parent. You're so irresponsible.' Naively, I'd hoped she'd be more understanding. What's a couple of days out of a lifetime after all?

I'll never have this time again. Looking out over the kitchen counter, over the countless food cartons and the empty beer bottles, I realise we've taken our time, been saying the goodbye that we didn't get to have. I hadn't realised how many memories you'd uploaded. I press my palm to the monitor.

'My, you're needy today, Sweets.'

Had anyone else said that I'd have been wounded, but you never put me down. With your teasing tone, I know you don't mean anything by it.

Finally, I had to pluck up courage. The question had been playing in my mind for hours; I'd palm the screen to ask and then lose my nerve, but now, now had to be the time. I wasn't sure if the estate agent would continue accepting my excuse that the house was taking longer than expected to pack up.

'Why? I want to know why you did it?'

'Did what, Sweets?'

'You know what I'm talking about.'

'Dinner? The bath? Or,' giggling, she whispers, 'you talking about that other thing? I thought you liked it.'

Bowing my head to the screen, 'Why'd you leave the kids and me?'

'Sweets, I'd never leave you.'

I can hear the pain in your voice. I know you mean it. You think you mean it. Chacha programmed this house at a time when she couldn't envision a world where she'd leave us. Herein lies the limitations of the programming. You only know what Chacha let you know. You're only as good as Chacha made you. Which means you'll never really be Chacha.

You understood this stuff better than me. I guess that's why you always got the work. You just seemed to gel with each new iteration of the tech while I was the hesitating Neanderthal in the background. The company saw what you had, pulling you up from the ranks of advertising until you were 'The Face'. My worries became nothing with you beside me.

The Houseplant was your brilliant idea. Our home, our beautiful big new home, was one of the first to launch the tech and we welcomed in Alectoria. As with everything, it was genius, our lives all the better for this new seamless integration. I never wanted to share you but before I knew it your voice, your brain and programming were filling homes all over the country.

It was all going alright. I didn't understand it, but it was going okay, until that night at the gym. I'd never come so close to losing everything. Never imagined I could be tempted by another woman. Jogging on the treadmill, I couldn't settle into my routine. I'd blink over and over, changing the landscape, changing the scenario, but I couldn't get in the zone. Zombie Apocalypse run down felt too aggressive, Lakeside Circuit too slow, my go-to, Savannah Sunset, didn't feel right.

Calling it quits, I tapped my wrist and the simulation stopped. That's when I saw you. You'd been running on the treadmill beside me. Beautiful blue-green eyes, full pouty lips, caramel skin and dark loose curls piled in a high ponytail. Only your fitness suit seemed out of touch, I'd never once seen you in pink.

'What are you doing here?' I'd asked. It wasn't like you to get in a workout in the evening, the morning was your focus time.

'Sweets, it's been a killer day. Killer year really. You and I need more time alone.'

Your voice seemed a little off kilter but then you had been running, so I put it down to being short of breath. 'Who's got the twins?'

'Don't panic, Sweets. I wrangled us some time.'

You winked and took my hand; it wasn't until I was soaping up some stranger's body in the shower cubicle that I realised it wasn't you. You hated cutesy tatts and that woman had a clover on her left hip. I'd never run so fast.

She laughed, now making no attempt to hide her own gravelly voice: 'So close. Come on now, she hasn't got anything that I don't have. What's the difference?'

'Sweets, it's only a real psycho that'd try and entrap you like that. Most people just purchase one or two features to enhance themselves. She must have been loaded to buy the whole makeup. As a matter of fact, I think you could make some extra cash, you're hot, I've always thought so.'

'But how? Your voice, your ideas, that's one thing but to sell *you*?' I was fuming. I couldn't stand that parts of you were out there on the bodies of strangers. I couldn't believe how calm you were about what had nearly happened.

'You've got it backwards. My body, it's not real, it's not constant. It won't always be like this.' You gestured down, as though inviting me to look. 'My ideas, however, my mind, that's the real me. And you know that better than anyone.'

'Yeah, but your voice and mind are in everyone's home now. That woman, she even spoke like you.'

That was the first time I realised I had been right to be scared. That was the moment I knew you didn't really know what you were doing.

Sitting on the cold marble benchtop in the desolate kitchen, I looked at my only companion, the Houseplant.

'You know where she is, don't you, Alectoria?' I grasp the pot in two hands. Telling myself I just intend to take it from the shelf, to discard it, but we both know that's not true. Not even possible. I feel it, pulsing in my palms, as though I grasped a beating human heart rather than the porcelain pot.

Pulse.

Pulse.

Pulse.

The plant is not like the interface screen. It lacks the familiarity of your voice, I should not be compelled to touch it, and yet, I try to pick it up. I can sense it anticipating my needs, my vulnerabilities, and like the opposite poles of a magnet I'm drawn in, knowing all the while that once I'm connected I won't be able to disconnect.

I feel the smoothness of the pot beneath my fingers. I somehow don't have the strength to lift it. Instead, I trace my hand up the pot through the soil and along the waxy tentacles. I feel the sparks, like static electricity, stinging my fingertips. Rather than repelling me, the sensation feels reassuring. It reminds me that I am alive and I can feel.

Beat.

Beat.

Beat.

I don't plug in. I don't need to. The Houseplant will take care of all my needs. One second we are separate entities and the next a tendril enters my uncovered port. On plugging in, my world goes white, my arms go limp, my body slackens.

I'll never need to worry over directing the flesh of my body again. I hear your voice one last time. 'It's so much better here, Sweets.'

Dolphin Dreaming

Vicky Daddo

The rippling funnel of moonlight highlighted spumy breakers. A salt-tang breeze whipped hair across her face, but pushing it away was as futile as pushing back on Luke. His tenacity was as ferocious as the ocean wind. It was one of the reasons she'd married him. Married. It made her sound so *settled*. And Natasha felt as far from that as she was from the horizon. She fiddled with the ring. A symbol of eternal love. An anchor.

She hadn't wanted to honeymoon at Haunted Hearts Bay, a blustery nook carved from granite. It sounded like bad luck. No, she'd dreamt of a secluded villa, margaritas and sunburn against satin sheets. But Luke. Luke had long told her of the legend of the silver dolphin and the good luck it brought. He'd insisted they take the Airbnb property that clung to the bluff so they could take brisk walks on crisp mornings to see Baru.

'That story is as old as the hills,' she'd laughed, flicking through travel magazines with images of azure waters and purple hibiscus, ostentatiously holding them up in front of him as he swatted them away in mock disgust.

But those legendary hills were still standing, still casting shadows and holding up trees. Myths persisted for a reason. Traditions and rituals continued because they grounded people, or made them feel like part of something bigger than their own small lives. Stories were shared because – no matter the generation, listening and learning – some themes were eternal and universal.

'Allow me to remind you how it goes,' he'd insisted, telling her the Dreamtime story of the children who'd defied their parents and gone in search of cool water on a hot day and ended up being dragged out to sea.

Luke used hand gestures and funny voices and dramatic pauses to embellish his narration. She could track the arc of the legend just from watching him, no sound required. He'd be a great dad, she often thought. So patient. Like a little boy himself.

'Boomali, the sea spirit, rescued them, but punished them for their disobedience by turning them into dolphins, never to see their families again.' His hand made a diving motion. 'What's the moral of the story, Nat?'

'Always carry water with you,' she'd say. Or, 'Keep your kids on one of those harnesses.' Or, 'Holiday inland.' Just to mess with him.

His answer was always the same. 'Don't cross the sea spirits.'

'Those poor parents,' Nat said the last time he told it, kissing the veins over the back of his hand.

He smiled up at her. 'Their sacrifice gave us dolphins, though. And if we see Baru, we'll have good fortune for the rest of our lives.'

'That's just white man's wishful thinking. An albino dolphin is rare and this one would have to be two hundred years old.'

He'd smiled his wonky grin. 'You've got to have dreams, Nat.'

Their dreams had led them directly to the Airbnb 'Beach View House'. Luke had renamed it Baru View House in his inimitable, optimistic way. Looking back at the bluff, she smiled to herself, mentally asking, 'Where's the bloody dolphin, Luke?'

She stayed on the beach a moment longer, the weight of the night vision goggles heavy around her neck. The strap scored her collar bones like Luke's whiskery jaw scraping the tender spots of her neck. His breath, like a conch shell, filled her ear.

Back at the house, the fire had gone out, leaving the darkened living room chilled. She should go back to bed, but the pull of the moonlight over the water was magnetic. She eyed the closed bedroom door, twirled her wedding ring and walked to the impressive floor-to-ceiling picture windows. In the near distance, a shape caught her attention. She blinked, believing herself too tired to be really seeing Baru. Still, she fumbled the goggles to her eyes hopefully and held her breath. Not a silver dolphin. A boat. A diver stood, plunged backwards into the ocean, didn't surface for a long time. She fell asleep on the sofa, woke with a cricked neck and a knot of disappointment in her stomach.

The next night, the full moon drew her back to the beach. Climbing over rusty boulders, she watched a tinny – the same one, she was certain – bumping over the water to shore, pulling up behind a clump of jagged rocks that glimmered in the strange light. The engine died and water slapped rhythmically in its place. She heard the diver humming a lilting, mournful tune as she crab-walked over the rocks to get a better look. Her breath caught in her throat as she saw what he was doing.

Deftly shucking the flesh from the shell with a small-bladed knife, he worked fast, scooping and discarding. Natasha realised the gleaming rocks were not rocks at all, but abalone shells piled high. His work was mesmeric and she hunkered down, wishing for Luke's strong arms wrapping around her to keep her warm.

She could hear Luke's intrigued tone. 'You know this is illegal, Nat. He's probably making squillions from this poaching. The Chinese black market is huge. But abalone. Ick! I've never acquired the taste. I'll take a cray any day. You, cray and a Chardonnay.'

He should be out here with her, sharing the grotesque fascination of the skill and skullduggery at play. She glanced back over her shoulder, picking out the faint glow of the fire up in the house. The poacher continued his shanty. Luke would probably introduce himself and ask to help, would learn the words to the song or make up his own lewder lyrics.

A splash from beyond the point. Natasha and the poacher snapped up their heads in unison, tracking the ripples. Another louder crash and she saw a movement, a tail maybe. Anticipation left her shaky and a fizz of emotion burst up into her throat. She hadn't brought the goggles, but the moon's glow was so bright it cast a silvery spotlight across the dark waters. It felt like destiny. Baru leapt and her silvery body curved over the water before diving under and up again, dancing in the streak of light.

'Holy shit!' The poacher raised his arms, clapped over his head.

Nat found herself grinning, wanting to join in with the stranger's applause. A warmth bloomed across her chest. Her heart beat as fast as it had when Luke whispered his vow of everlasting love. Without thinking, she stood up, ready to tell him, ready to hammer her husband's chest with her fists and say, 'I saw her. She was beautiful. So beautiful. You should have been here.'

Instead, as she stretched upwards, she twisted and overcorrected, breaking her fall with her left hand and a subdued 'oof'.

The diver dropped his knife and it clanged on the boat's deck. 'Who's there?'

Natasha held her breath but her wrist burnt with pain. She clamped her lips shut.

'I'm just here to see the dolphin,' the poacher said, his flippers thwacking the rock. Closer. Closer.

She nestled her injured hand against her chest and looked at the poacher's face, grooves from his scuba mask pitting his slick skin.

'I'm here to see the dolphin, too,' she said eventually, trying to keep her voice steady.

'You saw her?'

'I think so.'

'Good fortune forever,' he said, looking back at his catch.

'So the story goes.' Nat stood up, offering a conciliatory half-smile.

The poacher backed away, picked up an abalone. 'You want to try? I taught my son when he was a little tacker. In the end he was faster than me. All flash technique and that. But when he was just a boy, he was sloppy, left chunks of meat in the shell. I used to crack the shits at him and he'd yell back at me, you know? Then we'd do it all again.' His eyes shone in the unnaturally bright night. 'Funny what you miss the most when someone's gone. I miss his insults. I miss his mess.'

'I'm sorry,' she whispered, wondering what good fortune would bestow on this man if he'd already endured the worst loss.

The man shook his head. 'Long time ago now.' He offered her the knife.

She could hear Luke in her mind. 'Go on, Nat. It's our honeymoon. Push the boat out.' He would have laughed at his bad pun. She would have giggled in his wake. Instead, she felt the hot sting of tears, the throb in her wrist.

'I can't,' she croaked, lifting her hand. 'I think I've sprained it.'

'Here,' he said, pulling up a tea towel, arranging ice from the Esky in a circle in the centre before tying the cloth. He took her hand and placed it on the freezing bundle. 'Elevate it tonight. Rest.'

'After seeing the legendary Baru, I don't think I'll be sleeping much.'

The poacher turned to the open sea. 'My boy dreamt of seeing Baru. I told him it was rubbish, one of those urban myths. But secretly I told myself if I ever saw her, I'd jack this caper in. What d'you think? Was it a sign?'

Natasha thought of the dolphin, sleek, fluid and graceful; the polar opposite of Luke's papery skin, and jutting cheekbones as he'd rasped through their wedding vows. Of his insistence she go on the honeymoon anyway.

Luke's fingers had ringed her wrist. 'If you see that dolphin, let me go where she goes.' The very wrist that ached now. He'd given a weak squeeze. His last breath, his last act.

A sign.

The moonlight picked out the tiny notches patterned into her wedding band. A forget-me-not design etched into the precious metal. She twisted it round and round. An eternal loop.

'Swim,' she said to herself. 'Swim and dive and be free.'

It didn't feel like a sacrifice. It felt like a release, a letting go.

Baru made one last leap, so high she seemed to hang in the air, and Nat let her tears fall and fall.

Later, when the moon had slid away behind growing night clouds, and the poacher had disappeared into the blackness, she walked up the bluff, glad of the burn in her quads and the ache in her wrist. They distracted her from the pain in her heart.

Inside, the fire's embers glowed dully. Nat stoked the flames and they flickered, crackled back to life. The ring warmed on her finger, eliciting more weeping but also a broad smile and a gentle laugh. Somewhere out in the deep was a silver dolphin. Somewhere out there was her Luke.

Dying for Yum Cha

Bon-Wai Chou

Madame Leung-Kett still hankered for a good Chinese meal, even after fifty years in Australia. She was sitting at the kitchen table doing sums with an abacus while her sixteen-year-old granddaughter, Blanche, dusted, when she sprang to her feet and phoned her niece, Rosie, demanding she had better take her into town.

'I'll shout you a yum cha for your trouble,' she said. 'There are contagious diseases, I know, but you can't stay inside all day.'

When Rosie seemed to hesitate, Madame Leung-Kett bawled down the line, 'Paw! No Cantonese can go three months without their yum cha! How can you beat *har gow* and *siu mai* washed down with a good cup of *bo-lei* tea? You tell me!'

Madame Leung-Kett was determined to put her plan into action. She discussed the hundreds of types of succulent dumplings and dim sum, and just as Rosie started yearning for her favourite dish – *char siu bao* – Madame Leung-Kett hung up and began accosting her next victim.

'Now listen,' said the old woman to Blanche, who looked up from the furniture she was dusting. 'You're on school holidays so you can come too. The more people, the more variety. And *by gee*, the more cheaper!'

While waiting for her ride into town, Madame Leung-Kett decided to wash some dishes in a large saucepan, all the while reciting rambling thoughts to Blanche, who had come over to dry.

'He'd wear the same shirt till it went to holes, your Gong-Gong did, and eat overnight *soong* every day for lunch quite happily. But gawd, when he had yum cha, he'd empty every basket without a thought for anyone! His steamed sticky rice in lotus leaves meant everything to him. Paw! More than *me…*'

Blanche barely listened. Instead, she was thinking, *Por-Por is impossible. Every day I'm at her beck and call. If we're not rushing off to the first sitting of yum cha, I'm dragged to the safety box to check on her jewels and count King George V gold coins for the fiftieth time. When is me time? If I play conscripted domestic any longer, I'll go crazy! If only the old bag would shut her trap—*

Flushed with anger and agitation, Blanche tore off her jumper.

A shrill voice rang out, 'You'll catch your death in that!'

Blanche turned and saw her grandmother's eyes, bright and sharp, glued to the low-cut top stretched tightly over her young bosom.

'Exposing yourself like a cheap call girl. You've no shame!'

The old fool, Blanche thought, but she began to tremble, and words rushed out incoherently. 'No shame? What about *you*? Worrying yourself to death about a few cents, and washing up in two inches of water!'

'That's enough!' Madame Leung-Kett snapped. 'Can't I do as I please in my own house?'

'To the point of being ridiculous,' said Blanche, pointing indignantly at a piece of washed glad wrap hanging out to dry on the spout of the tap. 'You can't be serious about re-using this!'

Shame-faced, Madame Leung-Kett considered the forlorn, disfigured sheet of plastic, dripping with soapy water. 'What about it?' she said.

Blanche picked it up between her fingertips and flicked it into the air.

'Eh—' the old woman spluttered as the waterlogged missile landed smack in the middle of the rubbish bin. 'Paw! There's plenty life in that yet!' she shouted, striding to the bin to retrieve the soggy piece of plastic. 'That's the trouble with you modern young people. You don't know nothing! If you re-wash your glad wrap, your thirty-metre roll will last two, three years, I tell you, two, three years!'

'For God's sake, how long are you going to keep doing this?' said Blanche. 'It's not wartime.'

Madame Leung-Kett's eyes were wild.

'*Not wartime!*' she growled. 'I've been fighting every day for eighty years. And you tell me it's not wartime? Gawd, you young people know nothing!'

Blanche threw down the tea towel, but before she could storm off a car pulled up outside with a screech of brakes.

'By gee, she's here already.' Madame Leung-Kett grabbed her walking stick from the umbrella stand and headed out the front door.

The engine of the older-style Toyota Corona was throbbing. The woman inside was a fine-looking, middle-aged Eurasian, dressed in soft white flounces that fell in artistic folds, with her deep auburn hair immaculately groomed. Blanche opened the car door.

'Morning, Auntie Rose.'

'Good morning, Blanche. Good morning, Auntie Ivy. You look a million dollars.'

'Paw! You can talk, Rosie!' Madame Leung-Kett beamed, showing a mouthful of excellent dentures as she stepped into the front passenger seat, delighted her expensive English tweed suit had not gone unnoticed.

Blanche slid into the back seat and was nearly knocked out by the heady odour of jasmine perfume. She lowered the window.

'Hope it's not too windy for you,' she said.

'Oh, not at all,' said Auntie Rose. 'It's a lovely day for a drive and I'm really looking forward to the yum cha. It's been such a long time since I've had it.'

Rose backed out of the driveway and Blanche turned pale as the car raced menacingly down the hill, but Madame Leung-Kett was in high spirits.

'You know what, Rosie,' she said, launching straight into an account of her bargain-hunting exploits. 'I bought ten pig trotters for *a dollar* the other day at Coles. Can you believe that? And there's tomata for ninee-nine cents a kilo. Did you know that?'

Rose's mind was elsewhere, as she threaded her way erratically through the side streets, squealing tyres and tooting the horn as she went. Madame Leung-Kett continued undaunted.

'And there's a six-pack toilet paper going for a dolla-ninee-five. By gee, where can you get cheaper toilet paper? Stop at Coles, Rosie.'

The car bounced. Blanche gripped the grab handle tightly. Raising her eyes to the rear vision mirror she caught Rose staring ahead, hands stiff on the steering wheel, a 'don't disturb me' look in her eyes.

Another kilometre passed and Madame Leung-Kett's mouth was still bristling with prices.

'A dolla-ninee-five! I tell you, Rosie. Buy fifty rolls and you'll have enough for a year. Buy a hundred rolls and you'll—'

'You'll only save ten cents a roll,' Blanche interrupted.

Madame Leung-Kett took no notice. It was apparent she planned to demolish Coles of its entire stock of toilet paper.

'Buy two hundred and fifty rolls and you'll have enough to last five years. Store them in the garage, Rosie. They don't go off.'

'What about the petrol?' Blanche broke in. 'Where's the saving in that? And the time taken to drive out to woop woop—'

'Be quiet!' Madame Leung-Kett squawked. 'You're lucky to have me think of everything. Unless I'm on hand to attend to everything it all goes wrong. How else would you and your mother and father and sister live so well if it wasn't for me providing for you, thinking of everything? Did I tell you, Rosie, I've already fixed everything up for my funeral? I told the lawyer to put aside ten thousand dollars.'

Rose nodded, her face tense and her hands clutching the steering wheel more tightly.

'Yeah. But the gold lettering's not cheap,' Madame Leung-Kett went on, 'and I want it done properly. Deaths are costly, I tell you.'

'Don't start that again,' said Blanche.

'Look!' said Madame Leung-Kett. 'You should be thankful I bought the plot years ago when real estate was dirt cheap.'

'I know. I hear about it every day.'

'Well, Rosie hasn't heard it. Have you?'

'N-no,' said Rose without conviction, as she negotiated the last bend in the side street and emerged on the main road, narrowly missing a van.

'See! Just you listen and be quiet. I know all about the cost of dying, with your uncle, and your Gong-Gong going one after another. So, I planned ahead long ago and bought the plot next to your grandpa George. Prime Hong Kong real estate, I tell you, on the way to Stanley. Million-dollar sea view.'

'Who's going to see the view?' said Blanche, a smile creeping across her face.

Madame Leung-Kett lashed out at her. 'What did you say?'

'Nothing,' said Blanche.

'You all think old Por-Por know nothing! Well, I know all right. I know—'

'Could we have a bit of quiet, please?' said Rose. 'I'm trying to change lanes.'

'By gee, Rosie,' Madame Leung-Kett cut in. 'You got to learn to push in! How many times do I have to tell you? You have to stick your neck out to win.'

Blanche watched the rising needle of the speedometer with wide eyes, as Rose, goaded by her grandmother, bullied her way across three lanes of traffic. A kilometre later Madame Leung-Kett was still yelling in Rose's ear.

'Slowcoaches, that's the real disease in life, I tell you. All this smiling, waving, and shaking everybody's hands! You got to not care, Rosie. Now, how long till we get to Coles?'

Neither Rose nor Blanche said a word.

'You heard me?' said Madame Leung-Kett.

'You can forget about Coles,' said Blanche. 'You can't U-turn anywhere round here.'

Rose added, her voice faltering, 'I'm sorry, Auntie, but I really can't take you to Coles—'

'Paw! I don't believe that.'

'It's true, I can't do right-hand turns.'

Madame Leung-Kett's rage broke. 'No more excuses! We're not passing up a bargain like that for toilet paper—'

'Red light!' Blanche cried out.

Rose lifted her head. 'Oh, my God!'

The car screeched to a halt. The three women slumped forward. The pause seemed interminable until a voice squawked, 'Paw! Keep your eye on the road, Rosie.'

Rose, her armpits soaked, shifted gears. The car groaned uneasily. Blanche felt her body weight being thrown backwards and forwards. After a series of backfires and awkward jerks, Rose let out the clutch and the car leapt forward. They drove on in silence. Blanche was still feeling shaken when Madame Leung-Kett addressed her over her shoulder.

'That reminds me, if I die tomorrow—'

'Oh, Auntie, do you have to talk about this now?' Rose interjected.

'There'll be no cremation, you hear? Don't you dare have me burned. And the other thing you better understand straight away is I don't want none of those cheap rubber airlines flying me back to Hong Kong.'

'Rubber band airlines,' said Blanche.

'You laughing at me?' said Madame Leung-Kett.

'Never,' said Blanche, jerking forward as the gears changed.

Madame Leung-Kett bounced in her seat. 'By gee, Rosie, keep your eye on the road! Now hear this: after I'm dead and gone, don't start thinking you're rich, you hear? No point getting a lot of extravagant ideas. You still have to save and economise. You know I can't stand waste. That's why all the weight in my coffin cargo has got to be used up. It's all paid for. I paid for it! So, stuff in all you can, all the clothes and shoes you want to wear for my funeral and all the presents for the relatives. That way, when you lot come to Hong Kong, you'll have plenty of room in your check-in luggage. And make use of that hand luggage, you hear? I never have problems stuffing in at least six kilos in my handbag. How else d'you think I get to cross the gates with an extra ten kilos each time? I wear three singlets, two jumpers, two pairs of pants …'

Jesus, thought Blanche.

'Remember, I'm not going to die to help anyone. Especially not you lot! I know what you're all waiting for…'

Madame Leung-Kett spoke in a sharp bark for the next five minutes.

'Really, Auntie,' said Rose when Madame Leung-Kett finally came to a full stop. 'I don't know how you do it. I mean, all this planning and foresight. Blanche must learn a lot from you.'

'That's where you're wrong,' corrected Madame Leung-Kett. 'Mei-Mei has no idea.'

'What d'you mean?' Blanche shot back.

'You don't do *real* work. All you do is write.'

'What do you write?' asked Rose, glancing at Blanche, who made eye contact, then gazed out the window.

'Stories about *us*,' Madame Leung-Kett cut in. 'Spends hours at it, locked in her room. Just a waste of time. She'll go to jail for insulting others—'

Rose broke in, 'You never know, Auntie. Blanche might become rich and famous one day.'

'No money in what Mei-Mei does!' Madame Leung-Kett snapped.

Blanche decided it was time she said her piece, when Rose suddenly wailed, 'Oh, my God, I'm in the wrong lane! I can't do right-hand turns!'

A few feet away loomed a large intersection with cars hurtling at a terrifying rate.

'You have to go, Auntie Rose!' Blanche urged, seeing the traffic lights had already turned amber.

'But I *hate* right-hand turns!'

The cars waiting in front of them suddenly dashed across the road between the tiniest of gaps in the oncoming traffic. The next moment the lights turned red. Rose appealed to Blanche in the rear vision mirror.

'What am I going to do now?'

'Go!' yelled Blanche.

The car swerved halfway across the road then paused in the centre of the intersection. Blanche sprang forward in her seat, and shouted, 'You can't stop now!'

'But it's a red light.'

'You want to get us killed, Rosie!' Madame Leung-Kett roared.

Blanche turned her face sharply and saw four lanes of traffic advancing like a full battalion. She seized Rose by the arm.

'Go, for God's sake! Just go!'

The car leapt forward, screeching around the corner. The three women jerked acutely to the left then swerved back at a horrible angle.

'You – you both okay?' said Rose. Horns blared all around them.

Blanche couldn't speak or breathe. She was half on the floor, her heart pounding. Madame Leung-Kett was scrambling to clasp the dashboard.

'By gee, Rosie, I didn't want to die *today*!'

For a long time no one said a word.

I've got to get out of here, or I'll go mad! thought Blanche. Her mind was in overdrive when Rose jammed on the brakes again, tossing everyone forward.

'Paw!' said Madame Leung-Kett as she jerked her head back, indicating a vacant parking spot. 'You missed it, Rosie. That was perfect street parking.'

'It's a No Standing Zone,' said Blanche, losing patience, as she eyed the signposts through the window.

Rose looked nervously in the rearview mirror, her nose beaded with perspiration.

'Auntie,' she said timidly, as the car bucketed forward in the slow lane. 'I don't know if you know, but I can't reverse park.'

Madame Leung-Kett ignored the remark. 'Mei-Mei, keep your eye out for empty spots. Any will do. Oh look, there's one! Stop the car, Rosie. Mei-Mei, get out and stand there.'

'What?'

'I said, get out. If you stand there long enough, they won't stand in the way!'

Blanche tumbled out just as a sports car veered up alongside her. The driver sported tattoos, studs in the nose, and a look of brutality in his eyes.

'Eh! Ching-Chong. Get out the bloody way!'

The pumping music went up a notch, and the angry red machine leapt towards her. She skipped aside as the car ploughed its way into the tight spot. When it became obvious the vehicle was too long, the driver took off, leaving behind exhaust fumes and a finger jerking out of the window.

'Dickhead,' muttered Blanche as she watched the Corona reverse awkwardly into the narrow space. She hardly expected Auntie Rose would make it on her first attempt, but she managed to park without mishap.

Madame Leung-Kett stepped out at once with a tap of her stick. 'C'mon, Rosie. Get a move on. The first sitting's about to start.'

'Oh, Auntie—' Rose was sponging her forehead with a handkerchief.

'Come on, I'm starving!'

'Oh, Auntie. We'll never get there on time.'

Madame Leung-Kett hobbled with great vigour in the direction of Little Bourke Street. Blanche strode to catch up with the old woman as she crossed the road. A truck loaded with packages drove through a red light towards Madame Leung-Kett.

'Por-Por, stop!' Blanche shouted.

The old woman pointed her stick at the driver and swore, as the truck swerved round just avoiding her. Madame Leung-Kett shook her fist and shouted after the driver. Then she stopped.

Dozens of six-pack toilet paper were bouncing and bumping along the road. Auntie Rose, who was behind her, hurried forward.

'By gee!' Madame Leung-Kett exclaimed, seeing Rose eagerly grabbing the packages dislodged from the truck. 'You're a fast learner, Rosie!'

'Anything to avoid a right-hand turn, Auntie,' Rose beamed back at her, arms full.

It was eleven-thirty when they arrived at the Dragon Palace restaurant. A young waiter, perfectly dressed, led them to a table with a view.

'Not there! Outside the kitchen!' Madame Leung-Kett barked.

Two minutes later a server emerged with a trolley stacked high with piping hot bamboo steamers.

'Hey!' the old woman signalled from her commanding lookout.

The packets of toilet paper formed a citadel around their table as they downed their *har gow* and *siu mai*, before which, Madame Leung-Kett disinfected their rice bowls and chopsticks with hot *bo-lei* tea.

The Goat Came Back

Shaun Allen

The goat came back,
It wouldn't stay away.
The goat was on the doorstep the very next day.

It was a nursery rhyme from Stephen's childhood. One that his mother had sung to him about an evil man the day after New Year's Eve. The goat that the villagers had burdened with their years' sins and then chased out of the village with rocks and sticks, returned to that evil man who hadn't confessed all his sins and no matter what he did the goat returned to his doorstep every day until the man died of shame.

It was a nursery rhyme. It was a myth. And yet the goat was at this doorstep this morning, idly chewing on a nearby thistle. Its long fleece was matted with dirt and blood from yesterday's beating. The ear, that Stephen himself had grabbed and twisted, hung damaged over its face as it leaned down and cropped another prickly leaf from the plant. It looked at him as it chewed.

He waved his arms at it and ordered it to go away. He stamped his foot and shouted. It didn't move and ate another leaf. Nervously, Stephen looked up and down the street. It was early morning, light, but the sun had not yet cleared the mountains. No one in the village was stirring yet, last night's party had lasted well into the morning hours. No one was around to see the goat and the shame it would bring him.

Getting desperate Stephen kneeled in front of the goat and said, 'Okay, I confess. I didn't confess all my sins last night, but you understand right? Charles was right beside me and so was Felicity. I couldn't tell you that I had slept with Charles's wife while he was right there. The whole village was there, how was I to confess that? It was only the once.'

The goat continued to eat.

'Okay, you know now. I slept with another man's lawful wife. I had carnal relations with her and yes, I enjoyed it. But it's done okay. I confessed. You can go. I won't even hit you. No rocks. Okay?'

Stephen stood up and went back inside. He looked back at the grazing goat as he shut his door and prayed it would be gone when he returned.

It was gone when he checked later in the morning. Feeling incredibly relieved, he went about his daily tasks feeling less burdened like the other villagers, a jaunty skip to his step.

When he came home that night the goat was grazing in his kitchen, chewing on a pair of his pants. Stephen stared at it dumbly and then swallowed hard.

He edged his way past the goat, not taking his eyes from it and checked his back door. It was still secure; the locking bar he had dropped in place earlier this morning was still there. The elaborate and expensive lock he had bought from the city for his front door had been locked, he still held the key in his hand. Slowly, Stephen lifted the bar on the back door and opened it up. He walked back into the kitchen and up to the goat lifting a frying pan from a hook as he did. With a mighty swing he bought the pan down on the goat's rump. The goat bleated in alarm and bolted around the house smashing plates and ornaments before leaping out the open back door. Stephen raced to the door and slammed it dropping the bar firmly in place.

The next morning dawned fine and clear and Stephen lay in his bed half asleep as the sunlight touched his windows. He was bought to full wakefulness by an awful smell that seemed to be right beside him. He opened his eyes and there in the bed next to him was the goat, asleep on his sheets. Stephen jumped out of bed with a cry of alarm. He ran out of the room and slammed the door behind him. He chewed a knuckle while thinking and then slowly opened the door again; the goat was still asleep. He crept into the room and quietly got dressed and then left shutting and locking the door behind him again.

Outside a young boy walked past his house whistling softly to himself. An idea formed in Stephen's head, and he quickly penned a letter and raced outside.

'Young man!' he called for the boy who was now two houses down. 'Do you know Farley, the Furner?' The boy looked alarmed but nodded. 'A penny for you if you fetch this letter to him immediately.' Stephen held out the coin with the letter. 'Farley will have another for you when you deliver it.'

The boy eagerly grabbed the coin and letter and raced off down the street. Stephen returned inside his house and waited.

Farley arrived at the top of the next hour. Stephen ushered him in and quickly closed the door behind him.

'You owe me a penny, Stephen,' Farley announced as he entered.

'Blast your damn penny, Farley. We have a problem.' Stephen took his arm and led him to the bedroom door. He opened it without flourish and stepped aside.

Farley looked in and commented, 'You have a goat in your room.'

'Damn your eyes, you fool. I know there's a bloody goat in there. Look at the goat.'

Farley sighed and looked closely at the animal. 'Is that the scapegoat?' he said, astonished. His look turned to horror. 'What have you done? You bloody fool!'

Stephen stalked back into the foyer. 'You know these blasted country superstitions, man. What people do when the goat returns. My mother, bless her soul, told me the rhyme as a child but by the devil, I can't remember what happened to the fool afterwards. I told the damned goat my sin yesterday morning and sent it on its way hoping to be rid of the beast.' He waved his arm at the bedroom door.

Farley paced, running his hands through his grey hair. 'Not in my time has the goat ever returned. Not in my time. We must be rid of the beast.'

'Across the heath and into the forest, the old clearing where we … had our fun. Pray some damned wolf gets it or the devil does drag it down to hell. Dammit, Farley I left London to remove myself from scandal and now due to some pagan nonsense I may find myself embedded in it again.'

Farley walked to the lounge room followed by Stephen. 'We have to wait til night,' the baker said sitting on the couch. 'Has anyone seen it?'

'No.'

'You're sure?'

'Of course, I'm bloody sure,' Stephen snapped. 'I'd have the mob at my door if any fool had.'

'And you confessed everything you not told it the other night?'

'Yes. Everything about Charles's harlot wife. I had already confessed everything else.'

Farley raised an eyebrow at Stephen.

'Not that obviously! Dammit, Farley, I want to be rid of it all. That's why I came back.' Stephen sighed loudly and started to relax. 'If not for your help, Farley, I'd still be lost. I'm sorry for being so curt.'

'You're forgiven, lad. Your pants were always loosely tied. You're only trying to do the right thing now. We've a past, you and I. You're a good lad now. We'll tether the goat and at dusk lead it into the forest. For good measure we'll slit the beast's throat and bury it deep. You can handle a shovel still? London didn't make you soft did it, boy?'

Stephen smiled. 'You know I've dug my fair share of graves.' He looked at his hands. 'A blister never hurt anyone.'

The goat came back.
It wouldn't stay away.
The goat knows your thoughts when you go astray.

They waited until a few hours after dark to enter the bedroom and tether the goat. It accepted the rope without trouble and followed them sedately as they left the house out the back way and entered the laneway that led to the heath and the forest beyond.

At midnight they entered the trees and walked for an hour more to be sure they could not be seen from across the heath. They were being overly cautious, but Stephen didn't care. He walked confidently to a clearing he knew well and tied the goat to a fallen branch. Farley had bought a large knife from the kitchen and carried the spades that they would use to bury the animal.

Stephen put down his lantern and sat on the log near the tethered goat. Farley stabbed the spades into the ground and then sat next to him. He drew several deep, steadying breaths and then stood again and looked at the goat.

'Let's get this done,' Farley said. 'Take a spade. You still have that mean swing? You hit it and I'll cut its throat.'

Stephen nodded and stood up. He retrieved a spade and walked to the goat that looked at him with uninterested eyes. He lifted the spade up and as he swung down the goat bleated once and snapped the tether and ran into the forest. Stephen's swing hit the log with a crash and the vibration shuddered up his arm, forcing him to drop the spade and knocking him off his feet.

Farley rushed up to him.

'Go after the goat,' Stephen ordered, rubbing his numb arms.

Farley took off into the dark forest, following the trail of the goat.

Stephen shook his arms and cursed at his damned luck. 'What else could go wrong?' he muttered, then laughed to himself. 'Not much space left around here,' he said, looking around the clearing.

He knelt to pick up the spade when a shriek echoed through the trees.

'Farley?' Stephen laughed. 'Was that you? You squeak like a little mouse.' It was followed by a louder scream filled with pain. 'F … Farley?' Stephen whispered, trying to investigate the dark trees from his position. 'Farley, you prankster. Playing tricks on me? You know this place, Farley, the games we played here when we were younger.' There was only silence from the woods. 'Farley, no games now.' Stephen took a step towards the trees. He swallowed hard and took another step. There was silence from the woods, so he picked up a spade and his courage and walked slowly under the moon shadowed branches.

Stephen could find no sign of Farley in the immediate area.

'Farley, where are you, you bloody fool? If you're hiding and playing at some silly game, I'll bury in the clearing with all the other bastards whom we played with.'

At first the word was so soft that Stephen didn't even hear it over his own footfalls. Then it came louder so he had to strain his ears to make out the noise and then clearer still.

'Stephen.' It was whispered on the wind, carried through the trees and on the rustle of leaves.

Stephen turned to the sound of his name. Again, the soft echo of his name whispered through the pines and oaks and now a horrid smell assailed his senses.

When he turned again, he saw Farley on his knees and a horned devil holding him by the hair. Stephen screamed and stumbled backwards, tripping over his feet, and colliding with the ground. The spade tumbled from his hand. He cleared his vision with a shake of his head and looked up. Farley was still there but the beast was not.

'Farley, you fat fool. You scared me half to death.' Stephen sat up. Farley was shuddering, his hands over his face. 'Think that's funny, do you?'

Farley removed his hands and faced him. Stephen reeled, scrambling backwards. Farley had no eyes. Stephen could see that Farley's hands were dripping blood and his face was covered in it. Farley moaned and blood gushed from his mouth, stained his clothes and pooled between his legs. He vomited more blood than Stephen thought a man had and then coughed up more.

Stephen edged closer to his friend. 'Farley, you fool. I will get help.'

'Farley is doomed.' The voice was behind Stephen, deep and the words bleated out like a goat.

Stephen froze.

'But, you. You.' There were footfalls on the soft loam. 'Don't you see?'

Whatever it was reached its hand around Stephen. The other gripped his shoulder. The hand was three fingered, furred and cloven in appearance, but all Stephen saw was the eyes nestled in the palm. Farley's eyes.

Stephen felt the hot, fetid breath on his ear as the thing leaned close to him. He felt the soft tickle of its fur as it brushed his cheek and then it moved away and stepped in front of him. Behind the beast Farley, curled on his side like a baby, softly cried.

Stephen screwed his eyes shut. He shivered in the frigid air as sweat rolled down his forehead. There was no noise for some time and slowly Stephen opened his eyes. Patient as a goat, the beast was there. Covered in fine fleece, stained with blood and dirt, the beast regarded him with cocked head. The horns on its head curved backwards and from its snout it breathed slowly, the nostrils flaring with each breath.

It was the goat. The scapegoat. Now some twisted man shape and come to seek its vengeance. It regarded Stephen with dull eyes.

'I confessed,' Stephen managed to say, tremors shaking his voice. 'I told you everything.'

'Did you now?' The Scapegoat looked towards the clearing. 'Everything?'

Stephen turned his head in that direction. The clearing was where he and Farley used to play. 'No.' Stephen shook his head. 'That was just games. Farley did it all. He was always crazy like that.'

The Scapegoat regarded him with those vacant eyes.

'Farley always went first. Always had his fun first. He liked to hurt. He liked it when they cried.'

'Really?' The word was spoken slowly.

'I liked it to,' Stephen said softly. 'I laughed when they cried. I liked to humiliate them first.' Stephen grew angrier. 'I wanted them to beg. Beg me for their miserable lives. I wanted them dead! I did everything to take pain from their bodies as they begged for their useless existence.'

'Truth,' the beast said. 'At last.' The scapegoat dropped Farley's eyes and took Stephen's head in both hands.

Stephen started to weep. 'What are you?'

'Justice.' the Scapegoat said as Stephen's screams echoed through the still, midwinter air.

The goat came back,
It wouldn't stay away.
The goat waits in the forest to drag your soul away.

Little Victories

Tyler McPherson

Knock.

Knock.

Knock.

My knuckles smack against the wooden base of my bed for what feels like the hundredth time. I roll onto my back and look up at the ceiling praying that this is the last time that I have to do it. I shut my eyes, begging sleep to overwhelm me.

My brain is merciless. I feel the phantom touch of wood against my knuckles. The ghost of a knock. But it doesn't feel right. It just feels … incomplete.

'Shit.'

I lean over the side of my bed, feeling for the wooden base. Feeling frustration rise into me, I curl my fist again. Three times. It has to be three.

Knock.

Knock.

Knock.

When morning comes it is with tired eyes and sore hands. My stomach roils with shame and something I almost don't recognise. Disappointment. It is something I have learnt to live with. I try, and fail, to push it from my mind as I get up.

I wish breakfast was quieter. But when you have a brother and sister who constantly fight over pretty much anything, everything is just *loud*.

'Lewis, have your breakfast. The bus will be here in ten minutes!' Mum shouts over the twins squabbling over the cornflakes. Her dark hair is pushed back and she wears bright yellow gloves. She adds the sound of clinking dishes to the cacophony.

I slide a piece of bread into the toaster and try to slip off to the bathroom. My sister, Abbie, one half of the dynamic duo that is my twin siblings, stands in my way.

'Nope, you got up too late. I need to brush my teeth.' She fills the small hallway with her small body, her pink pyjamas slightly offsetting her stubborn expression.

'I need a shower.'

'We have ten minutes. That's not even enough time with how long you take.'

It's probably true. It's my biggest environmental impact. But for ten minutes, my brain is aligned with my body. I can forget about my knocking, about the anxiety beating in the back of my mind. Everything is just calm.

'Fine,' I sigh. Fighting with her (or my brother for that matter) is just not worth it.

'Maybe if you stopped playing games so late, you'd beat her there,' Byron, part two of the dynamic duo, unhelpfully chimes in.

'I wasn't pla— What?' I manage to spit out.

'I heard you banging,' he says. 'I could hear you playing games, although by the sounds of it you weren't playing games well.' He smiles, cornflakes smeared across his teeth, but I don't have time to be disgusted.

He'd heard the knocks.

My bedroom shares a wall with that of the twins, I know that. But they are normally asleep well before I go to bed. Well before the knocking starts. And I tried to be quiet, but apparently not quiet enough.

I gape for a moment, my brain trying to come up with a response—an excuse—that is believable. I come up blank.

'Whatever.' I hurry back into my room before he can say anymore.

I try to reign in my nerves as I get ready for school. My hands tremble slightly with the panic.

He just thinks it is video games, I tell myself. *He doesn't know.*

But he could and that scares me more than I like to admit.

'Lewis!' Mum calls through the door tearing me from the spiral I was heading down. 'Bus is two minutes away! You're going to be late.'

Most kids don't like school. I see it as a welcome distraction, something that takes my mind away from the constant knot in my stomach.

'Right, sorry. Leaving now.' I swing my backpack over my shoulder and open the door. 'Bye, Mum.'

I can see the bus already pulled into the bus stop, the twins boarding. My friend is stalling the bus driver and his face breaks into relief when he sees me arrive.

'Sorry,' I pant out to the disgruntled driver.

'This is the last time, Lewis,' he grumbles.

Carson and I find a seat right at the front. Ours is the last stop and so there are never many empty spots. It's better this way. The people at the back are loud and obnoxious. I'd rather sit away from them.

'How was your night?' he asks.

My brain briefly skips back to my knocking episode. I just shrug and reply, 'Just played some games. Nothing much really. I completely forgot about my homework, though. What about you?'

'I forgot too.'

An easy silence strikes up between the two of us as we travel. Seeing each other every day takes away the need for constant conversation. I open my book and he flicks in earbuds, each losing ourselves to our thoughts until the bus arrives at school.

Our common room has a couch that we like to call the 'therapy couch'. It isn't more than a small ratty two-seater with half the stuffing showing, but whoever claims it gets to spread out right across the thing, while anyone else has to sit in the armchair beside. Carson and I are nearly always the first ones there.

I race across the room and literally throw myself onto the couch turning and smiling to my friend.

'Suck it,' I say.

'Seems fair. You would be the one of us that most needs therapy,' he snipes back at me. I don't tell him that he is probably right.

The school bell announces the arrival of first period and I grab my books from the locker. Biology. Great. My worst subject. Worst of all is that none of my friends are in my class. Instead, the class is full of people who actually know what is going on. I barely know what the lymphatic system is: today's class topic.

'Lymph nodes are found throughout many key areas of your body,' Ms Tonic drones on as though reading from the textbook. 'You can find them under the armpits, in the neck and in the groin. They can swell when you get sick or have an infection. Normally this symbolises nothing, but sometimes cancer can also cause the lymph nodes to swell. This is fairly uncommon so hopefully none of you will experience it. Touch wood.'

She raps small bony fingers against oak. A gentle drumbeat to end her monologue.

I was starting to lose focus during her discussion, losing myself in the lull of her voice. But those words jolt me awake. I feel my fingers curl into fists and quickly force them into my pockets. I don't need to do that. Not here. I don't have cancer.

But what if I do? What if cancer has been building inside me for years and I will only find it now that I knew what to look for?

No. I don't believe that.

What about my friends and family? What if they have cancer? I should knock on wood just in case.

I try to order my thoughts as they slowly blossom inside. My concentration is gone. I try to read the words on the board, to listen to Ms. Tonic but it's too late. My world narrows until I can't hear anything over the word pounding in time with my heartbeat.

Cancer.

Cancer.

Cancer!

It is too loud to ignore. My arm is in the air before I know it and Ms Tonic calls my name out.

'Can I please go to the bathroom?'

She rolls her eyes and, with a quick glance at the clock, waves me out.

I power-walk through the empty school towards the toilets. No one is inside. That is good. Locking myself into a cubicle, I put the lid down and sit on it, drawing in a deep breath. Okay. This isn't good. I open the notes section on my phone and type in the word 'cancer'. I've found keeping track of what triggers me to panic helps to focus my attention.

I start a new line.

I don't have cancer.

I read it once. Then again. Then a third time, trying to sear the memory of those words into my brain.

Okay, but what if …?

My parents do not have cancer. Carson does not have cancer. I do not have cancer.

My mouth moves with the words. A chant on a sliver of breath hoping to make it stick. But only one words stays.

Cancer.

Cancer.

Cancer!

The battle is already lost and I know it. I can already feel the way the wood would brush against my knuckles. Hard. Comforting. Real. I peek out the cubicle door double-checking no one is there. All clear. Then I graze my knuckles three times on the back of the door. Then again. And again.

Grey flecks of paint peel off the wood. I watch as they drift towards the ground, waiting for the feeling of calm, for everything to feel *right* again. It doesn't come.

Again.

BANG!

My heart, and my body, leap into the air as the bathroom door slams. I freeze, hand still clenched into a fist, teeth gritted as footsteps cross the room to the urinal. A shadow crosses beneath the cubicle door. Had they heard me knocking? Had they heard me whispering? Did they even care?

My pulse is pounding. Thump, thump, thump. A steady rhythm. Calming. My hand itches to follow that beat, knuckles craving mahogany.

Don't do it. Don't do it. Don't do it. I silently tell myself.

Cancer. Cancer. Cancer. My mind responds.

I bite my lip, not daring to breathe, even though I know that whoever is out there can't see me. Can't hear the thoughts overtaking my mind.

With a deep sigh and a flush, the footsteps retreat and a closing door signals their exit.

My breath comes out in a rush and almost involuntarily my hand reaches forward to touch the reassuring wood of the cubicle door.

Again. And again.

Frustration builds in me as the action repeats over and over, I feel tears sting my eyes and curses whisper from my lips. Finally, I smack my knuckles into the wood three times. I hit the wood hard enough to break the skin. The pain tells me it is done right.

Calm slips through me. It's okay. The ritual has been completed and I'm safe. Carson is safe. My parents are safe.

But as the calm settles down, the tempest begins to swirl. I feel my cheeks redden in embarrassment at myself and shame burns the corners of my eyes. What is wrong with me? Why am I like this?

I know I need to stop. This has been going on for too long. I know in the logical part of my brain that this ritual does nothing. All it does is make me feel better. And that is a slippery slope. I need to try harder. I *will* try harder.

I open the door and return to class.

'What happened to your hand?'

These are the first words Carson says to me when I sit opposite him at lunch. I look down at the ragged tears across my knuckles and the sharp red that flashes through. I shove my hands into my pockets.

'Nothing.' *Lie*.

'Doesn't look like nothing?'

'Honestly, I jammed it in the biology room door after class.' *Lie*.

'Should you get it checked out?'

'Nah, it's alright.' *Lie*. 'I'll just chuck a few Band-Aids on it when I get home.'

Now I was lying to my friends. Convincingly, it seems as Carson just shrugs, takes another bite of his sandwich and then continues on with his story about how he had managed to skip English Lit for the third time this week.

'It's easy, I just say I need to study in the library. No distractions, so I can prepare for next week's essay. Mrs Lenehan doesn't suspect a thing.' He takes another bite of his sandwich and looks at me with a concerned expression. 'You sure your hand is okay?'

'Yeah, why's that?'

'You just look a little pale is all. Maybe you should go see the nurse?'

'It is fine.' *Lie*

Sixth period. Final class of the day.

Carson sits where he always does in my classes; to my right. I secretly pass him my phone. It's his turn at *Angry Birds*. Mr Lachlan is trying to sound inspired about the difference between the purpose of an article and its contention or some other writing technique that I know I am never going to understand by end of year exams.

The afternoon has been good. Art, then history. Two favourite subjects in a row. If it wasn't for the dull ache in my knuckles, I would have temporarily forgotten about this morning's incident.

Temporarily. It wouldn't be far from my mind in forty minutes when the school bell rings.

'Thirty-five,' Carson whispers to me.

'What?'

'Thirty-five minutes to home time,' he crosses out a number written in the corner of his page and scribbles in the new time. His countdown to the end of the worst class ever.

'Carson. Lewis. Am I boring you?'

I jerk my head up to the board feeling my heart fall as the words there do not give me any insight into the past five minutes discussion.

'No. We're good,' the words tumble from my lips before I think about them and I almost groan aloud. I know what is coming next.

'Then perhaps you can answer the question I just asked the class?'

My mind fumbles to grab hold of what had just been said.

'I don—'

'The contention is what the author is trying to say,' Carson cuts over me.

Mr Lachlan looks at him and nods, his glasses slipping down his nose a little.

'Correct. Try and pay attention, Lewis. As I was saying today, we are going to be doing a practice analysis. I have a pile of different articles and I want you all to clearly identify the items that I have listed here.'

He points at the list of words I don't understand. This is going to be a long class. Mr Lachlan starts handing around pieces of paper. Mine lands in front of me face-down and I flip it over to get a head start on the work.

'MOBILE PHONES AND CANCER! THE TRUTH REVEALED.'

I feel dizzy. Mr Lachlan is still talking but I can't hear him anymore, Carson beside me is just a blur in the corner of my vision.

Cancer.

My whole arm tingles, fingers curling and uncurling against my leg as my brain is thrown into overdrive. It's a warning. A sign. Twice in one day, the world is trying to tell you something. Listen. You're in danger. Danger! DANG—

'Your turn, bro.' I feel Carson press against my arm, grounding me back to the present moment. He slides my phone onto my leg, warm against my shorts. Almost hot.

Phone. Cancer. Phone. Cancer. Cancer. Phone. Leg.

I jerk my knee, letting the phone tumble to the floor with a gentle bump. Carson turns at the sound.

'Your phone,' he whispers.

'I know,' my eyes are fixed on the sheet of paper in front of me. 'If I get it now, Mr Lachlan will notice. It can wait until after class, sorry.' *Lie.*

'Damn,' he whispers back but doesn't push it. He remains unaware of the beat inside my head. Unaware of the way my hand is curled into a fist on the table beside my article. Unaware of the gritting of my teeth.

I will not knock.

Seconds that feel like hours slip by until it has been a minute.

Then two.

Then three.

After five, I let my eyes drift back to the article. Six and I start reading. I shake my head almost imperceptibly every time I skim over the word 'cancer', trying to loosen the word's grip in my mind. But its claws run deep.

Fifteen minutes since the urge started and I still haven't knocked. This must be a personal best. I glance at Carson who is head down, his pen hastily scratching across the surface of his page. I pick up my own.

Thirty minutes and, mercifully, the bell rings and in the chaos of books slamming shut and pencil cases zipping closed I smack my fist against the wooden table lightly.

Knock.

    Knock.

        Knock

I bend down and pick up the now defused cancer bomb that is my phone.

I feel light as I settle into the night-time rhythm. I've kept the beast at bay once today; maybe I can do it again.

I read my notes as I brush my teeth, hoping that the memory of already performing the ritual will stop the compulsion from rising inside of me.

No luck.

As I slide under the covers, *what ifs* begin to crowd in on my thoughts.

What if you don't knock tonight and you get cancer? Or your parents or Byron or Abbie or Carson or your friends or Ms Tonic or what if one of them dies or has an accident or gets sick or one of their friends and family gets injured or …

The relentless cycle grows inside of me and my nails bite into my palms. I succeeded in fighting back the compulsion once today. I can do it again. I will do it again. I'm not giving in this time.

I distract myself with thoughts of Carson. I picture myself in the 'therapy chair' telling him all about these little incidents. I wonder what he would say if I told him that I did this for him. That I was scared he would be hurt if I didn't.

I can clearly picture the worry that would briefly wash over his face before he relaxes back into his joker self.

'Lewis, what are you worrying about me for? I'm going to live forever.' Imaginary Carson winks at me. 'Plus you aren't magic, although that would be cool, you can't stop the world from being the world.'

I let the image go. My fingers loosen, but the need is still there.

I think of my parents and the twins and realise they would tell me similar. That I am not magic. My knocks won't affect them. The only person I am hurting is myself.

I decide then that I will beat this. I will find a professional. Seek help. Be the person I want to be. Free from this anxiety.

For a second, my thoughts clear. The fog lifts. There has to be another way. What am I thinking?

But then the flash of sunlight disappears beneath a cloud as a spasm runs through fingers that ache to brush against wood. My mind races to compel me. I wiggle my fingers to shake the compulsion from then. When that doesn't work, I roll onto my stomach and shove them under my pillow.

Whatever happens I'm not going to knock tonight. Just one night. It's a small goal. A first step.

But an achievable one. I lie and listen to the sounds of my clock as I wait for exhaustion to take over and pull me into sleep.

I can do this.

Tick.

    Tick.

        Tick.

Author Bios

Shaun Allen hails from Ngunnawal country and spent seven years living in tropical North Queensland. A military history buff, self-confessed nerd, and amateur gardener, he has either his head in a book, mind on a video game or hands in the dirt. He has been writing for more years than he can remember and has been an active member in many writing groups, most recently The Inner North Scribblers.

Katrina Burge is a word nerd and writer who holds an Associate Degree in Professional Writing and Editing at RMIT University. She spends her time developing her manuscripts and freelance editing for several publishing houses. She blogs at katrinaburge.wixsite.com/writer, where she reviews books and video game soundtracks. Her work has been published in *Rise: An Anthology* and *Catalyst Magazine*.

Daniel T. Car is a Melbourne-based writer, graduate of RMIT's Associate Degree of Professional Writing and Editing, and editor with *The Write Stuff Melbourne*. He believes that not all ghosts and ghouls commit evil and that not all evils are committed by ghosts and ghouls. Daniel hopes his writing, however dark, might add some magic and vibrance to the world.

Bon-Wai Chou (she/her) is an Australian Chinese writer born in Chicago but raised in Hong Kong and Melbourne. Her stories and memoirs have been awarded by *Glimmer Train* and *Writer's Digest*, longlisted for the *Bridport Short Story Prize*, published in *Southerly, Meanjin, The Age* and anthologised in *Roots: Home Is Who We Are*, among others. A descendant of Queensland gold rush immigrants, she is currently working on a novel-in-stories.

Vicky Daddo lives in Hazelwood South, Victoria. She is Writers Victoria Regional Ambassador for Gippsland and President of the Gippsland Writers Network. She programs the Latrobe Literary Festival. Her short fiction has appeared in *The Big Issue, Women's Day, That's Life* and several anthologies. Competition credits include the Rachel Funari Prize, Hope Prize and Scarlet Stilettos. Her unpublished novels have been selected for QWC/ Hachette Manuscript Development program and Adaptable.

Mick Davidson has a professional writing career stretching back forty-five years and encompassing newspaper and magazine journalism, technical writing, poetry, short stories, novels and lyrics. When not mentally editing airport signage or lamenting the misuse of words, he can be found cycling around metro Melbourne and Mornington Peninsula, and paddleboarding.

Rosemary Dickson was born, bred and lives with her partner of twenty-five years in Melbourne, on Wurundjeri country. Retired from a varied career, including cemetery labourer, postie and public servant, she likes to read, write, swim, see friends and family, and travel. Rosey has studied Italian, Linguistics and writing, and enjoys being a member of Inner North Scribblers. In 2019 *n-Scribe* magazine published one of her short stories.

Jane Downing (she/her) lives and writes in Wiradjuri country. She has stories and poetry published around Australia and overseas, including in *Griffith Review, The Big Issue, Antipodes, Southerly, Westerly, Island, Overland, Meanjin, Canberra Times, Cordite,* and *Best Australian Poems* (2004 & 2015). In 2016 she was shortlisted for the Commonwealth Short Story Prize. Her novel, *The Sultan's Daughter,* was released by Obiter Publishing in 2020. She can be found at janedowning.wordpress.com.

J.A. Gleeson holds a Bachelor of Arts and a Master of Creative Writing, Publishing and Editing from the University of Melbourne. She has been published in *Voiceworks, Room Magazine* and *F*EMS Zine,* and tends to write about the non-nuclear home and mental health. When she isn't writing, Jamisyn can be found binge-reading and drinking her body weight in oat milk lattes.

Megan Howden lives on Wurundjeri country. She enjoys perusing the shelves of second handbook stores, walking in nature and playing with her two energetic children. Having an eclectic taste in reading, Megan finds the short story the ideal medium for her to explore different writing styles and genres. Megan is a proud member of the writers' group, Inner North Scribblers, and has previously had short stories published in *n-SCRIBE* magazine.

Tyler McPherson is an author and editor currently living in Melbourne, Australia. He is passionate about stories in all their forms. Tyler primarily writes fiction, and he has had several short stories published both locally and internationally. Some of Tyler's work can be seen in *Verandah 30* and Deakin University's *WORDLY*.

Anna Miller (she/her) lives in Melbourne but grew up in the surrounding Dandenong Hills. She is a musician and keen advocate for quality music education for children; her writing to date has mostly taken the form of composition and songwriting for children. *At the End of the Rainbow* is her first published story for 'grown-ups'.

Nancy Podimane has spent equal time in Melbourne and Rome, and enjoys writing about the dilemma of misunderstandings, the frustration of expectations and the ordeal of separations. She trained as a teacher and has never given up working with children, teaching English as a foreign language. Currently living in a bungalow in Richmond leading a minimalist life, with the occasional transgression.

Ben Redwood began writing in high school but only recently began sharing his work outside of his family and friendship group. A previous story of his was published in the 2021 *Hammond House Publishing Anthology*. He lives in Melbourne with his cat, Alexis. When not writing, he works full-time for the state government, and otherwise enjoys basketball, reading, and streaming binges.

Seth Robinson is the author of *Welcome to Bellevue* (Grattan Street Press, 2020). His creative works have featured in publications including *Everything, All at Once*, *Aurealis Magazine*, *Intermissions*, and the *University of Sydney Anthology*, among others. Seth is currently working on his next novel, and on completing his Doctor of Arts (Creative Writing) through the University of Sydney. You can find out more about Seth and his work at www.sethrobinson.ink

Natalie A. Vella is an award-winning Australian writer of Sri Lankan/Maltese background with awards for her short story writing. Her memoir and feature articles have been published in ABC News, *Neos Kosmos* and *SBS Life*. Passionate about podcasting, her non-fiction podcast, *Memoria*, reached the finals of the 2019 Australian Podcast Awards. When not writing, she is in her garden.

Pinion Press is an imprint of Busybird Publising.

We specialise in publishing a handful of our own titles yearly, trying to combine quality and enjoyability with some altruistic outcome, e.g. raising awareness for a particular condition (as our glorious coffee table photography book, *Walk With Me* – a journal of Kev Howlett's trek up to Mount Everest Base Camp and back – raised awareness of Charcot-Marie-Tooth disease), and/or donate a portion of proceeds for books to various foundations, such as Women Helping Other Women, Breast Cancer Victoria, the Prostate Cancer Foundation, the Epilepsy Foundation, Vision Australia, and the Indigenous Literacy Foundation.

Busybird Publishing is a boutique micropublisher based in the heart of Montmorency, Victoria.

We help authors self-publish. A fee-for-service self-publisher, we make no claims on rights or royalties, and are determined to make sure our authors have a pleasurable, gratifying, and educational journey.

We also run workshops on various forms of writing (fiction, nonfiction, memoir), publishing, and photography, organise writing retreats; host a monthly Open Mic Night (the third Wednesday of every month); and hold competitions to help aspiring writers get published or win mentoring.

To learn more about Busybird Publishing, check out our website at www.busybird.com.au.